A Toast to the Gloom

"Gentlemen," said Skeeve disguised as King Rodrick, "what are your opinions of my bride-to-be?"

"The words 'cold-blooded' and 'ruthless' come to mind," the general said, "and that's the impression of a man who's made a career of the carnage of war."

"I'm sure that the rumors that she murdered her father are exaggerated," Grimble argued weakly. . . .

HIT OR MYTH
Robert Asprin

ACE BOOKS, NEW YORK

HIT OR MYTH

An Ace Book / published by arrangement with
Starblaze Editions of The Donning Company/Publishers

PRINTING HISTORY
Donning edition / 1983
Ace edition / September 1985

ISBN: 0-441-33851-8

Ace Books are published by The Berkley Publishing Group,
200 Madison Avenue, New York, New York 10016.
The name "ACE" and the "A" logo
are trademarks belonging to Charter Communications, Inc.

PRINTED IN THE UNITED STATES OF AMERICA

20   19   18   17   16   15   14   13   12

Chapter One:

PERHAPS if I hadn't been so preoccupied with my own thoughts when I walked into my quarters that day, I wouldn't have been caught unawares. Still, who expects to get caught in a magikal attack just walking into their own room?

Okay, okay! So I *am* the Court Magician of Possiltum, and maybe I *have* been getting a bit of a reputation lately. I still should be able to walk into my own room without getting jumped! I mean, if a magician isn't safe in his own quarters, can he be safe anywhere?

Scratch that question!

It's the kind of thing my teacher says to convince me that choosing magic for a career path is not the best way to insure living out one's normal life span. Of course, it doesn't take much convincing. Actions speak louder than words, and the action since I signed on as his apprentice has been loud enough to convince me that a magician's life is not particularly quiet. I mean, when you realize that within days of meeting him, we both got lynched by an angry mob . . . as in hung by the neck . . .

But I digress.

We started out with me simply walking into my room. Yeah, simple! There was a demon waiting for me, a Pervect to be exact. This in itself wasn't unusual. Aahz, the teacher I mentioned earlier, is a Pervect. In fact, he shares my quarters with me. What *was* unusual was that the demon waiting for me wasn't Aahz!

Now I haven't met many Pervects . . . heck, the only one I know is Aahz . . . but I know Aahz very well, and this Pervect wasn't him!

This demon was shorter than my mentor, his scales were a lighter shade of green, and his gold eyes were set closer together. What's more, he wasn't smiling . . . and Aahz always smiles, even when he's mad . . . *especially* when he's mad. To the average eye Aahz and this stranger might look alike, but to me they were as different as a Deveel and an Imp. Of course, there was a time when I couldn't tell the difference between a Deveel and an Imp. It says something about the company I've been keeping lately.

"Who are you?" I demanded.

"You Skeeve?"

"Yeah. Me Skeeve. Who you?"

For an answer, I suddenly felt myself snatched into the air by an invisible hand and spun end over end until I finally stopped dangling head down four feet off the floor.

"Don't get smart with me, punk. I understand you're holding a relative of mine in some kind of bondage. I want him back. Understand?"

He emphasized his point by lowering me to within a few inches of the floor, then using that surface to rap my head sharply.

I may not be the greatest magician ever, but I knew what he was doing. He was using his mind to levitate me about the room. I've done it myself to small objects from time to time. Of course, it occurred to me that I wasn't a small object and that I was dealing with someone a bit better versed in the magikal arts than myself. As such, I deemed it wiser to keep my temper and my manners.

"You know Aahz?"

"Sure do. And I want him back."

The latter was accompanied by another head rap. So much for holding my temper.

"Then you should know him well enough to know that nobody holds him against his will!"

My head started for the floor again, but stopped short of its target. From my inverted position I could get a partial view of the demon tapping himself thoughtfully on the chin.

"That's true," he murmured. "All right. . . ."

I was turned into an upright position once more.

". . . Let's take it from the top. Where's Aahz, and what's keeping him in this backwater dimension?"

"I think *and* talk better with my feet on the ground."

"Hmm? Oh! Sorry."

I was lowered into a normal standing position. Now that I was self-supporting again, I realized the interrogation had left me with a splitting headache.

"He's back in General Badaxe's quarters arguing military tactics," I managed. "It was so boring I came back here. He should be along soon. They were almost out of wine when I left."

"Tactics and wine, eh?" my visitor grimaced. "That sounds like Aahz. What's the rest of it? Why is he staying around a nowhere dimension like Klah and how did he get mixed up with the Great Skeeve?"

"You've heard of me?"

"Here and there around the dimensions," the demon

acknowledged. "In some circles they think you're pretty hot stuff. That's why I started wondering if you'd managed to cage Aahz somehow. I was braced for a real battle royale when you walked in."

"Well, actually I'm not all that good," I admitted. "I've only really started making headway in the last couple years since I started studying under Aahz. I'd still be a total nothing if he hadn't lost his powers and taken me on as an apprentice."

"Bingo!" my visitor declared, holding up his hand. "I think you just explained everything. Aahz lost his powers and took on a new apprentice! No wonder he hasn't been home in a while. And all this talk about the Great Skeeve is just a standard Aahz-managed hype job for a new talent. Right?"

"We *have* taken on a few rough assignments," I said defensively.

"In which Aahz choreographed, then set you up to take the credit. Right?"

"What's 'choreographed'?" I asked. Obviously the family similarity was more than scale deep.

"Well, I hope you're up to operating on your own, Skeeve, 'cause I'm taking your mentor back to Perv with me."

"But you don't have to rescue him from me!" I protested. "He's free to come and go as he wants."

"I'm not saving him from you, I'm saving him from Aahz. Our colleague has an overblown sense of responsibility that isn't always in his own best interest. Do you know how lucrative a practice he's letting fall apart on Perv while he clowns around with you?"

"No," I admitted.

"Well, he's losing money every day he's gone . . . and that means the family is losing money."

Right there I gave up the argument. Early on in my

association with Aahz I learned the futility of trying to talk a Pervect out of money. The fact that Aahz was willing to sacrifice a steady income to work with me was an incredible tribute to our friendship . . . or his sense of duty. Of course, there's more than one way to win an argument.

"Well, as I said before, I can't keep him here," I said innocently. "If you can convince him he's not needed any more. . . ."

"No way, punk," the demon sneered. "We both know that won't get him to desert an apprentice. I'm going to lure him back to Perv with a blatant lie. And *you're* going to keep your mouth shut."

"But . . ."

". . . Because if you don't, I'll make sure there's nothing left to keep him in Klah . . . meaning you! Now before you even think about trying to match magik with me, remember something. *You've* been studying under Aahz for a couple years now. *I* graduated after over three hundred years of apprenticeship. So far, I'm willing to live and let live. You should be able to earn a living on what you've learned so far, maybe even pick up a few new tricks as you go along. *However*, if you cross me now, there won't be enough of you to pick up with a sponge. Do we understand each other?"

I was suddenly aware why nobody we met in our dimension-crawling ever wanted to tangle with a Pervect. I was also aware that someone had just walked into the room behind me.

"Rupert!"

"Uncle Aahz!"

The two pounded each other on the back. I gave them lots of room.

"Hey kid, this is my nephew Rupert . . . but I see you've already met."

"Unfortunately," I grumbled.

That earned me a black look from Rupert, but Aahz missed it completely.

"So what brings you to Klah, nephew? A bit off your normal prowl pattern, isn't it?"

"It's Dad. He wants you."

"Sorry," Aahz was suddenly his normal self again. "I've got too many irons in the fire here to get drawn into some family squabble."

"But he's dying."

That stopped Aahz for a moment.

"My brother? Nonsense. He's too tough to kill. He could even beat me in an unfair fight."

"He got into a fight with Mom."

A look of concern crossed Aahz's face. I could see he was wavering.

"That serious, huh? I don't know, though. If he's really dying, I don't see what I can do to help."

"It shouldn't take long," Rupert urged. "He said something about his will."

I groaned inwardly. Trust a Pervect to know a Pervect's weaknesses.

"Well, I guess my business here can keep for a few days," Aahz declared with false reluctance. "Stay out of trouble, kid. I'll be back as soon as I can."

"Let's get going," Rupert suggested, hiding his triumphant grin. "The sooner we get to Perv, the sooner you can be back."

"But Aahz. . . ."

"Yeah, kid?"

I saw Rupert's brow darken.

"I . . . I just wanted to say 'goodbye.' "

"Hey, don't make a big thing of this, kid. It's not like I was going forever."

Before I could respond, Rupert clapped an arm

around Aahz's shoulder and they both faded from view.
  Gone.

  Somehow I couldn't make myself believe it had happened. My mentor had been spirited away . . . permanently. Whatever I had learned from Aahz would have to do, because now I was totally on my own.

  Then I heard a knock at my door.

Chapter Two:

"When things are blackest, I just tell myself 'cheer up, things could be worse!' And sure enough, they get worse!"

—SKEEVE

I DECIDED that as Court Magician of Possiltum, my response should be gracious.

"Go away!"

That *was* gracious. If you knew what my actual thoughts were, you'd realize that. Very few people ever visited me in my chambers, and I didn't want to see any of them just then.

"Do you know who you're talking to?" came a muffled voice from the other side of the door.

"No! And I don't care! Go away!"

"This is Rodrick the Fifth. Your King!"

That stopped me. Upset or not, that title belonged to the man who set and paid my wages. As I said earlier, I *have* learned a few things from Aahz.

"Do you know who *you're* talking to?" I called back, and hoped.

There was a moment's pause.

"I assume I'm talking to Skeeve the Magnificent, Court Magician of Possiltum. At best, he'll be the one to bear the brunt of my wrath if I'm kept waiting outside his chambers much longer.''

So much for hoping. These things never work in real life the way they do in jokes.

Moving with undignified haste, I pounced on the door handle and wrenched it open.

"Good afternoon, Lord Magician. May I come in?"

"Certainly, Your Majesty," I said, standing aside. "I never refuse a fifth."

The King frowned.

"Is that a joke? If so, I don't get the point."

"Neither do I," I admitted calmly. "It's something Aahz my apprentice says."

"Ah, yes. Your apprentice. Is he about?"

Rodrick swept majestically into the room, peering curiously into the corners as if he expected Aahz to spring forth from the walls.

"No. He's . . . out."

"Good. I had hoped to speak with you alone. Hmmm . . . these are really quite spacious quarters. I don't recall having been here before."

That was an understatement. Not only had the King never visited my room in his palace, I couldn't recall having seen him when he wasn't either on the throne or in its near vicinity.

"Your Majesty has never graced me with his presence since I accepted position in his court," I said.

"Oh. Then, that's probably why I don't recall being here," Rodrick responded lamely.

That in itself was strange. Usually the King was quite glib and never at a loss for words. In fact, the more I thought about it, the stranger this royal visit to my private chambers became. Despite my distress at Aahz's unplanned and apparently permanent departure, I felt my curiosity beginning to grow.

"May I ask the reason for this pleasant, though unexpected audience?"

"Well . . ." the King began, then shot one more look about the room. "Are you sure your apprentice isn't about?"

"Positive. He's . . . I sent him on a vacation."

"A vacation?"

"Yes. He's been studying awfully hard lately."

The King frowned slightly.

"I don't remember approving a vacation."

For a moment, I thought I was going to get caught in my own deception. Then I remembered that in addition to the various interdimensional languages, Aahz had also been teaching me to speak "bureaucrat."

"I didn't really feel your authorization was necessary," I said loftily. "Technically, my apprentice is not on your Majesty's payroll. I am paying him out of *my* wages, which makes him my employee, subject to my rules including vacations . . . or dismissal. While he is subject to your laws, as is any subject of Possiltum, I don't feel he actually is governed by Subparagraph G concerning palace staff!"

My brief oration had the desired effect: it both confused and bored my audience. Aahz would have been proud of me. I was particularly pleased that I had managed to sneak in that part about dismissals. It meant that when Aahz didn't return, I could claim that I had dismissed him without changing the wage paid me by the crown.

Of course, this got me brooding again about Aahz not coming back.

"Well, whatever. I'm glad to see your philosophy regarding vacations mirrors my own, Lord Magician. Everyone should have a vacation. In fact, that's why I came to see you this afternoon.''

That threw me.

''A vacation? But your Majesty, I don't need a vacation.''

That threw the King.

''You? Of course not. You and that apprentice of yours spend most of your time gallivanting around other worlds. You've got a lot of nerve asking for a vacation.''

That did it. All the anger I had been storing up since Rupert's arrival exploded.

''I didn't *ask* for a vacation!''

''Oh! Yes. Of course.''

''And furthermore, that 'gallivanting around other worlds' you mentioned is stock in trade for magicians, court or otherwise. It enables us to work our wonders . . . like saving your kingdom from Big Julie's army. Remember?''

''How could I forget. I . . .''

''If, however, your Majesty feels I have been lax in fulfilling my duties as his court magician, he need only ask for my resignation and it's his. If he recalls, *he* approached *me* for this position. I didn't ask for *that* either!''

''Please, Lord Magician,'' Rodrick interrupted desperately, ''I meant no offense. Your services have been more than satisfactory. In fact, any reluctance I expressed regarding your vacation was based on a fear of having to run the kingdom for a period without your powers available. If you really feel you want a vacation, I'm sure we could work out something to . . .''

''I don't *want* a vacation. All right? Let's drop the subject.''

''Certainly. I just thought . . . very well.''

Shaking his head slightly, he headed for the door.

Winning the argument put me in a much better mood. After the beating my ego had taken from Rupert, it was nice to hear *someone* say they thought my powers were worth something.

It occurred to me, however, that winning the argument with the man who paid my wages might not have been the wisest way to bounce back.

"Your Majesty?"

The King stopped.

"Aren't you forgetting something?"

He frowned.

". . . Like the original reason for your visit? Since I wasn't asking for a vacation, and you weren't offering one, I assume you had something else on your mind?"

"Oh, yes. Quite right. But all things considered, this might not be the time to discuss it."

"What? Because of our misunderstanding? Think nothing of it, your Majesty. These things happen. Rest assured I am still your loyal retainer, ready to do anything in my power to assist you in the management of your kingdom."

As I said before, I was getting pretty good at shoveling when the situation called for it.

Rodrick beamed.

"I'm glad to hear that, Master Skeeve. That is precisely why I came to you today."

"And how may I be of service?"

"It's about a vacation."

I closed my eyes.

For a brief moment, I knew . . . *knew*, mind you . . . how Aahz felt. I knew what it felt to be sincerely trying to help someone, only to find that that someone seems bound and determined to drive you out of your mind.

The King saw my expression and continued hastily, "Not a vacation for you. A vacation for me!"

That opened my eyes. Figuratively and literally.

"You, your Majesty? But Kings don't take vacations."

"That's the whole point."

Rodrick began pacing the floor nervously as he spoke.

"The pressures of being a King mount up like they do on any other job. The difference is that as a King you never get a break. No time to rest and collect your thoughts, or even just sleep late. From the coronation when the crown hits your head until it's removed by voluntary or forcible retirement, you are the King."

"Gee, that's tough, Your Majesty. I wish there was something I could do to help."

The King stopped pacing and beamed at me again.

"But you can! That's why I'm here!"

"Me? I can't approve a vacation for you! Even if it were in my power, and it isn't, the kingdom needs a king on the throne all the time. It can't spare you, even for one day!"

"Exactly! That's why I can't leave the throne unattended. If I wanted a vacation, I'd need a stand-in."

An alarm bell went off in my mind.

Now, however much Aahz may have nagged me about being a slow student, I'm not stupid. Even before I met Aahz . . . heck, before I learned my letters . . . I knew how to add two and two to get four. In this case, one two was the king's need for a stand-in; the second two was his presence in my quarters, and the four was. . . .

"Surely your Majesty can't mean me!"

"Of course I mean you," Rodrick confirmed. "The fact is, Lord Magician, I had this in mind when I hired you to your current position."

"You did?"

I could feel the jaws of the trap closing. If this was indeed why the King had hired me, I would be ill-advised to refuse the assignment. Rodrick might decide my services were no longer needed, and the last thing I needed with Aahz gone was to get cut off from my source of income. I wasn't sure what the job market was like for ex-court magicians, but I was sure I didn't want to find out first hand.

"As you said earlier, the powers of the Court Magician are at my disposal, and one of the powers you demonstrated when we first met was the ability to change your own shape, or the shape of others, at will."

The disguise spell! It was one of the first spells Aahz had taught me and one of the ones most frequently used over our last several adventures. After all the times it's bailed me out of tight spots, who would have guessed it would be the spell to get me into trouble? Well, there *was* the time it had gotten me hung. . . .

"But, your Majesty, I couldn't possibly substitute for you. I don't know how to be a King!"

"Nothing to it," Rodrick smiled. "The nice thing about being a King is that even when you're wrong, no one dares to point it out."

"But. . . ."

"And besides, it will only be for one day. What could possibly go wrong in one day?"

Chapter Three:

"Once a knight, always a knight,
But once a King is once too often!"
— SIR BELLA OF EASTMARCH

Now, I don't want you to think I'm a pushover. I drove a hard bargain with the King before giving in. I not only managed to get him to agree to a bonus, but to cough up a hefty percentage in advance before accepting the assignment. Not bad for a fledgling magician who was over a barrel.

Of course, once I accepted, I was no longer over a barrel, I was in over my head!

The more I thought about it, the worse the idea of standing in for the King seemed. The trouble was, I didn't have a choice . . . or did I? I thought about it some more and a glimmer of hope appeared.

There was a way out! The only question was, how far could I run in a day? While not particularly worldly (or off-worldly for that matter) I was pretty sure that double-crossing kings wasn't the healthiest of pastimes.

It was going to be a big decision, definitely the biggest I ever had to make on my own. The King (or to be exact, his stand-in) wasn't due to make an appearance until noon tomorrow, so I had a little time to mull things over. With that in mind, I decided to talk it out with my last friend left in the palace.

"What do you think, Gleep? Should I take it on the lam, or stick around and try to bluff it out for one day as king?"

The response was brief and to the point.

"Gleep!"

For those of you who've tuned in to this series late, Gleep is my pet. He lives in the Royal Stables. He's also a twenty-foot long blue dragon . . . half grown. (I shudder to think what he'll be like when he's fully grown! Groan!) As to his witty conversation, you'll have to forgive him. He only has a one-word vocabulary, but he makes up for it by using that word a lot. Wordy or not, I turned to him in this moment of crisis because with Aahz gone, he was the only one in this dimension who would be even vaguely sympathetic to my problem. That in itself says a lot about the social life of a magician.

"Come on, Gleep, get serious. I'm in real trouble. If I try to stand in for the King, I might make a terrible mistake . . . like starting a war or hanging an innocent man. On the other hand, if I double-cross the King and disappear, you and I would spend the rest of our lives as hunted fugitives."

The unicorn in the next stall snorted and stamped a foot angrily.

"Sorry, Buttercup. The *three* of us would be hunted fugitives."

War unicorns aren't all that common, even in Royal Stables. That particular war unicorn was mine. I acquired him as a gift shortly after I acquired Gleep. As I said before, this life-style is more than a little zooish.

"In a kingdom with a bad king, a lot of people would get hurt," I reasoned, "and I'd be a terrible king. Heck, I'm not all that good a magician."

"Gleep," my pet argued sternly.

"Thanks for the vote of confidence, but it's true. I don't want to hurt anybody, but I'm not wild about being a hunted fugitive, either."

Tired of verbalizing his affection, Gleep decided to demonstrate his feelings by licking my face. Now, aside from leaving a slimy residue, my dragon's kisses have one other side effect. His breath is a blast of stench exceeded only by the smell of Pervish cooking.

"G . . . Gleep, old boy," I managed at last, "I love you dearly, but if you do that twice a week, we may part company . . . permanently!"

"Gleep?"

That earned me a hurt expression, which I erased simply enough by scratching his head. It occurred to me that dragons had survived because each of them only became emotionally attached to one being in its lifetime. If their breath reached the entire population instead of a single individual, they would have been hunted into extinction long ago. No, it was better that only one person should suffer than . . .

Another part of my mind grabbed that thought and started turning it over.

"If I run, then I'll be the only one in trouble, but if I try to be king, the whole kingdom suffers! That's it! I have to leave. It's the only decent thing to do. Thanks, Gleep!"

"Gleep?"

My pet cocked his head in puzzlement.

"I'll explain later. All right. It's decided. You two stock up on food while I duck back to my room to get a few things. Then it's 'Goodbye, Possiltum!' "

I've had pause to wonder what would have happened if I'd followed my original plan: just headed for my room, gathered up my belongings, and left. The timing for the rest of the evening would have changed, and the rest of this story would have been totally different. As it was, I made a slight detour. Halfway to my room, Aahz's training cut in. That is, I started thinking about money.

Even as a hunted fugitive, money would come in handy . . . and the King's advance would only last so long. With a little extra cash, I could run a lot farther, hide a lot longer . . . or at the very least live a lot better. . . .

Buoyed by these thoughts, I went looking for J. R. Grimble.

The Chancellor of the Exchequer and I had never been what you would call close friends. Blood enemies would be a better description. Aahz always maintained that this was because of my growing influence in court. Not so. The truth was that my mentor's greed for additional funding was surpassed only by Grimble's reluctance to part with the same. Literally the same, since my wages came out of those coffers so closely guarded by the Chancellor.

I found him, as expected, in the tiny cubicle he used for an office. Scuttlebutt has it he repeatedly refused larger rooms, trying desperately to impress the rest of the staff by setting an example of frugality. It didn't work, but he kept trying and hoping.

His desk was elbow deep in paper covered by tiny little numbers which he alternately peered at and changed while moving various sheets from stack to stack. There were similar stacks on the floor and on the only other available chair, leading me to believe he had been at his current task for some time. Seeing no available space for sitting or standing, I elected to lean against the door frame.

"Working late, Lord Chancellor?"

That earned me a brief, dark glare before he returned to his work.

"If I were a magician, I'd be working late. As Chancellor of the Exchequer, these *are* my normal hours. For your information, things are going rather smoothly. So smoothly, in fact, I may be able to wrap up early tonight, say in another three or four hours."

"What are you working on?"

"Next year's Budget and Operating Plan, and it's almost done. That is, providing someone doesn't want to risk incurring my permanent disfavor by trying to change a number on me at the last minute."

The last was accompanied by what can only be described as a meaningful stare.

I ignored it.

I mean, what the heck! I was already on his bad side, so his threats didn't scare me at all.

"Then it's a good thing I caught you before you finished your task," I said nonchalantly. "I want to discuss something with you that will undoubtedly have an impact on your figures. Specifically, a change in my pay scale."

"Out of the question!" Grimble exploded. "You're already the highest paid employee on the staff, including myself. It's outrageous that you would even think of asking for a pay increase."

"Not a pay *increase*, Lord Chancellor, a pay cut."

That stopped him.

"A pay cut?"

"Say, down to nothing."

He leaned back in his chair and regarded me suspiciously.

"I find it hard to believe that you and your apprentice are willing to work for nothing. Forgive me, but I always distrust noble sacrifice as a motive. Though I dislike greed, at least it's a drive I can understand."

"Perhaps that's why we've always gotten along so well," I purred. "However, you're quite right. I have no intention of working for free. I was thinking of leaving the court of Possiltum to seek employment elsewhere."

The chancellor's eyebrows shot up.

"While I won't argue your plan, I must admit it surprises me. I was under the impression you were quite enamored of your position here in 'a soft job,' I believe is how your scaly apprentice describes it. What could possibly entice you to trade the comforts of court life for an uncertain future on the open road?"

"Why, a bribe, of course," I smiled. "A lump sum of a thousand gold pieces."

"I see," Grimble murmured softly. "And who's offering this bribe, if I might ask?"

I stared at the ceiling.

"Actually, I was rather hoping that *you* would."

There was a bit of haggling after that, but mostly on the terms of our agreement. Grimble *really* wanted Aahz and me out of his accounts, though I suspect he would have been less malleable if he had realized he was only dealing with me. There was a bit of name calling and breast beating, but the end result is what counts, and that end result was my heading for my quarters, a thousand gold pieces richer in exchange for a promise that it was the last money I would ever receive from Grimble. It was one more reason for my being on my way as soon as possible.

With light heart and heavy purse, I entered my quarters.

Remember the last time I entered my quarters? How there was a demon waiting for me? Well, it happened again.

Now don't get me wrong. This *isn't* a regular oc-currence in my day-to-day existence. One demon show-ing up unannounced is a rarity. Two demons . . . well, no matter how you looked at it, this was going to be a red-letter day in my diary.

Does it seem to you I'm stalling? I am. You see, this demon I knew, and her name was Massha!

"Well hel-lo, high roller! I was just in the neighbor-hood and thought I'd stop by and say 'Hi!' "

She started forward to give me a hug, and I hastily moved to put something immobile between us. A 'hi!' and a hug might not sound like a threat to you. If not, you don't know Massha!

I have nothing against hello hugs. I have another demon friend named Tananda (yes, I have a *lot* of demon friends these days) whose hello hugs are high points in my existence. Tananda is cute, curvaceous, and cuddly. Okay, so she's also an assassin, but her hello hugs can get a rise out of a statue.

Massha, on the other hand, is *not* cute and cuddly. Massha is immense . . . and then some. I didn't doubt the sincere goodwill behind her greeting. I was just afraid that if she hugged me, it would take days to find my way out again . . . and I had a getaway to plan.

"Um . . . Hi, Massha. Good to see you . . . all of you."

The last time I had seen Massha, she was disguised as a gaudy circus tent, except it wasn't a disguise. It was actually the way she dressed. This time, though, she had apparently kicked out the jams . . . along with her entire wardrobe and any modicum of good taste. Okay, she wasn't completely naked. She was wearing a leopard-skin bikini, but she was showing enough flesh for four *normal* naked people. A bikini, her usual wheelbarrow full of jewelry, light green lipstick that clashed with her orange hair, and a tattoo on her bicep. That was Massha. Class all the way.

"What brings you to Klah? Aren't you still working Jahk?" I asked, mentioning the dimension where we met.

"The boys will just have to work things out without me for a while. I'm on a little . . . vacation."

There was a lot of that going around.

"But what are you doing here?"

"Not much for small talk, are you? I like that in a man."

My skin started to crawl a little on that last bit, but she continued.

"Well . . . while I'm here, I thought I'd take another little peek at your General Badaxe, but that's not the real reason for my visit. I was hoping you and me could talk a little . . . business."

My life flashed before my eyes. For a moment, neither Aahz's departure nor the King's assignment was my biggest problem . . . pun intended.

"Me?" I managed at last.

"That's right, hot stuff. I've been giving it a lot of thought since you and your scaly green sidekick rolled through my territory, and yesterday I made up my mind. I've decided to sign on as your apprentice."

Chapter Four:

"Duty: A fee paid for transacting in good(s)."

— U.S. DEPT. OF COMMERCE

"BUT your Majesty, he promised me he'd pay the other half before spring, and . . ."

"I did not."

"Did too."

"Liar!"

"Thief!"

"Citizens," I said, "I can only listen to one side at a time. Now then, you! Tell me what you remember being said."

That's right. *I* said. There I was, sitting on the very throne I had decided to avoid at all cost.

Actually, this king business wasn't all that rough. Rodrick had briefed me on basic procedure and provided me with a wardrobe, and from there it was fairly simple. The problems paraded before me weren't all that hard to solve, but there were lots of them.

At first I was scared, then for a while it was fun. Now it was just boring. I had lost count of how many cases I had listened to, but I had developed a new sympathy for Rodrick's desire to get away for a while. I was ready for a vacation before lunch rolled around. It was beyond my comprehension how he had lasted for years of this nonsense.

You may wonder how I went from talking with Massha to sitting on the throne. Well, I wonder myself from time to time, but here's what happened as near as I can reconstruct it.

Needless to say, her request to work as my apprentice caught me unprepared.

"M . . . my . . . but Massha. You already *have* a job as a court magician. Why would you want to apprentice yourself to me?"

In response, Massha heaved a great sigh. It was a startling phenomenon to watch. Not just because there was so much of Massha moving in so many different directions, but because when she was done, she seemed to have deflated to nearly half her original size. She was no longer an imposing figure, just a rather tired looking fat woman.

"Look, Skeeve," she said in a low voice that bore no resemblance to her normal vampish tones. "If we're going to work together, we've got to be honest with each other. Court magician or not, we both know that I don't know any magik. I'm a mechanic . . . a gimmick freak. I've got enough magik baubles to hold down a job, but any bozo with a big enough bankroll could buy the same stuff at the Bazaar at Deva.

"Now, mind you, I'm not complaining. Old Massha's been kicked around by some of the best and nobody's ever heard her complain. I've been happy with what I have up to now. It's just when I saw you and your rat pack put one over on *both* city-states at the Big Game with some *real* magik, I knew there was something to learn besides how to operate gimmicks. So whattaya say? Will you help me learn a little of the stuff I really got into the magik biz for?"

Her honesty was making me more than a little uncomfortable. I wanted to help her, but I sure didn't want an apprentice right now. I decided to stall.

"Why did you choose magik for a profession, anyway?"

That got me a sad smile.

"You're sweet, Skeeve, but we were going to be honest with each other, remember? I mean, look at me. What am I supposed to do for a living? Get married and be a housewife? Who would have me? Even a blind man could figure out in no time flat that I was more than he had bargained for . . . a lot more. I resigned myself to the way I look a long time ago. I accepted it and covered up any embarrassment I felt with loud talk and flamboyant airs. It was only natural that a profession like magik that thrives on loud talk and flamboyant airs would attract me."

"We aren't *all* loud talk," I said cautiously.

"I know," she smiled. "You don't have to act big because you've got the clout to deliver what you promise. It impressed me on Jahk, and everyone I talked to at the Bazaar on Deva said the same thing. 'Skeeve doesn't strut much, but don't start a fight with him.' That's why I want you for my teacher. I already know how to talk loud."

Honesty and flattery are a devastating one-two punch. Whatever I thought about her before, right now Massha had me eating out of the palm of her hand. Before I committed myself to anything I might regret later, I decided to try fighting her with her own weapons.

"Massha . . . we're going to be honest with each other, right? Well, I can't accept you as an apprentice right now for two reasons. The first is simple. I don't know that much magik myself. No matter what kind of scam we pull on the paying customers, including the ones on Deva, the truth is that I'm just a student. I'm still learning the business myself."

"That's no problem, big bwana," Maasha laughed, regaining some of her customary composure. "Magik is like that: the more you learn, the more you find there is to know. That's why the really big guns in our business spend all their time closeted away studying and practicing. You know *some* magik, and that's some more than I know. I'll be grateful for anything you're willing to teach me."

"Oh." I said, a bit surprised that my big confession hadn't fazed her at all. "Well, there's still the second reason."

"And that is?"

". . . That I'm in a bit of trouble myself. In fact, I was just getting ready to sneak out of the kingdom when you showed up."

A small frown wrinkled Massha's forehead.

"Hmm . . ." she said, thoughtfully. "Maybe you'd better give me some of the details of this trouble you're in. Sometimes talking it out helps, and that's what apprentices are for."

"They are?" I countered skeptically. "I've been apprenticed twice, and I don't remember either of the magicians I studied under confiding in me with their problems."

"Well, that's what *Massha's* for. Listening happens to be one of the few things I'm *really* good at. Now give. What's happened to put a high-stepper like you on the run?"

Seeing no easy alternative, I told her about the King's assignment and my subsequent deal with Grimble. She was right. She was an excellent listener, making just enough sympathetic noise to keep me talking without actually interrupting my train of thought.

When I finally wound down, she sighed and shook her head.

"You're right. You've got a real problem there. But I think there are a few things you've overlooked in reaching your final decision."

"Such as . . . ?"

"Well, first, you're right. A bad king is worse than a good king. The problem is that a bad king is better than no king at all. Roddie Five is counting on you to fill his chair tomorrow, and if you don't show up, the whole kingdom goes into a panic because the king has disappeared."

"I hadn't thought about it that way," I admitted.

"Then there's the thing with Grimble. We all pick up a little extra cash when we can, but in this case if it comes out that Grimble paid you to skip out when the King was counting on you, *his* head goes on the chopping block for treason."

I closed my eyes.

That did it. It was bad enough to hurt the faceless masses, but when the mass had a face, even if it was Grimble's, I couldn't let him face a treason charge because of my cowardice.

"You're right," I sighed. "I'm going to have to sit in for the King tomorrow."

"With me as your apprentice?"

"Ask me after tomorrow . . . if I'm still alive. In the meantime, scurry off and say 'Hello' to Badaxe. I know he'll be glad to see you."

"Your Majesty?"

I snapped back to the present, and realized the two arguers were now looking at me, presumably to render a decision.

"If I understand this case correctly," I stalled, "both of you are claiming ownership of the same cat. Correct?"

Two heads bobbed in quick agreement.

"Well, if the two of you can't decide the problem between you, it seems to me there's only one solution. Cut the cat in two and each of you keep half."

This was supposed to inspire them to settle their difference with a quick compromise. Instead they thanked me for my wisdom, shook hands, and left smiling, presumably to carve up their cat.

It occurred to me, not for the first time today, that many of the citizens of Possiltum don't have both oars in the water. What anyone could do with half a dead cat, or a whole dead cat for that matter, was beyond me.

Suddenly I was very tired. With an offhanded wave I beckoned the herald forward.

"How many more are waiting out there?" I asked.

"That was the last. We deliberately kept the case load light today so your Majesty could prepare for tomorrow."

"Tomorrow?"

The question slipped out reflexively. Actually, I didn't really care what happened tomorrow. My assignment was done. I had survived the day, and tomorrow was Rodrick's problem.

"Yes, tomorrow . . . when your bride arrives."

Suddenly I was no longer tired. Not a bit. I was wide awake and listening with every pore.

"My bride?" I asked cautiously.

"Surely your Majesty hasn't forgotten. She specifically scheduled her arrival so that she would have a week to prepare for your wedding."

Case load be hanged. Now I knew why dear Rodrick wanted a vacation. I also knew, with cold certainty, that he wouldn't be back tonight to relieve me of my duties. Not tonight, and maybe not ever.

Chapter Five:

"The only thing worse than a sorcerer is a sorcerer's apprentice."

—M. MOUSE

FOR once, I successfully suppressed the urge to panic. I had to! Without Aahz around to hold things together until I calmed down, I couldn't afford hysterics.

Instead, I thought . . . and thought.

I was in a jam, and no matter how I turned it over in my mind, it was going to take more than just me to get out of it.

I thought of Massha.

Then I thought about suicide.

Then I thought about Massha again.

With firm resolve and weak knees, I made my decision. The question was, how to locate Massha? The answer came on the heels of the question. Standing in for the king had been nothing but a pain so far. It was about time I started making it work *for* me for a change.

"Guard!"

A uniformed soldier materialized by the throne with impressive speed.

"Yes, your Majesty?"

"Pass the word for General Badaxe. I'd like to see him."

"Umm . . . begging your Majesty's pardon. He's with a lady just now."

"Good. I mean, bring them both."

"But . . ."

"Now."

"Yes, your Majesty!"

The guard was gone with the same speed with which he had appeared.

I tried not to grin. I had never gotten along particularly well with the military of Possiltum. Of course, the fact that my first exposure to them was when Aahz and I were hired to fight their war for them might have something to do with it. Anyway, the thought of some poor honor guard having to interrupt his general's *tête-à-tête* was enough to make me smile, the first in several days.

Still, sending a guard to fetch the person I wanted to see was certainly better than chasing them down myself. Perhaps being a king *did* have its advantages.

Two hours later, I was still waiting. In that time, I had more than ample opportunity to reconsider the benefit of issuing kingly summons. Having sent for Badaxe, I was obligated to wait for him in the throne room until he appeared.

At one point I considered the horrible possibility that he had taken Massha riding and that it might be *days* before they were located. After a little additional thought, I discarded the idea. There wasn't a steed in the Kingdom, including Gleep, who could carry Massha more than a few steps before collapsing.

I was still contemplating the image of Massha, sitting indignant on the ground with horse's legs protruding grotesquely from beneath her rump, when the herald sprang into action.

"Now comes General Badaxe . . . and a friend."

With that, the man stood aside. Actually, he took several sideways steps to stand aside.

I've already described Massha's bulk. Well, Hugh Badaxe wasn't far behind her. What he lacked in girth, he made up for in muscle. My initial impression of the General remained unchanged; that he had won his rank by taking on the rest of the army . . . and winning. Of course, he was wearing his formal bearskin, the clean one, which made him appear all the larger. While I had been there when they met, I had never actually seen Badaxe and Massha standing side by side before. The overall effect was awe-inspiring. Together, they might have been a pageant of a barbarian invasion gone decadent . . . if it weren't for the General's axe. His namesake, a huge, double-bitted hand axe, rode comfortably in its customary place on the General's right hip, and the glitter from it wasn't all decorative. Here, at least, was one barbarian who hadn't let decadence go to his sword arm.

"Your Majesty."

Badaxe rumbled his salutation as he dropped to one knee with an ease that denied his size. One could almost imagine the skull of a fallen enemy crackling sharply beneath that descending knee. I forced the thought from my mind.

"Greetings, General. Won't you introduce me to your . . . companion?"

"I . . . certainly, your Majesty. May I present Massha, Court Magician of Ta-hoe, and friend of both myself and Lord Skeeve, Magician to your own court here at Possiltum."

"Charmed, your Majesty."

I realized with a start that Massha was about to attempt to imitate Badaxe by dropping to one knee. Even if she were able to execute such a maneuver, it would require sufficient effort as to invite ridicule from the other court retainers present . . . and somehow I didn't want that.

"Ah . . . there is no need for that," I asserted hastily. "It was not our intention to hold formal court here, but rather an informal social occasion."

That caused a minor stir with the court, including the general who frowned in slight puzzlement. Still, I was already committed to a line of conversation, so I blundered on.

"In fact, that was the only reason for the summons. I wished to meet the lady dazzling enough to lure our general from his usual position by my side."

"Your Majesty gave his permission for my absence today," the general protested.

"Quite right. As I said, this is a social gathering only. In fact, there are too many people here for casual conversation. It is our wish that the court be adjourned for the day and the room cleared that I might speak freely with this visiting dignitary."

Again there was a general ripple of surprise, but a royal order was a royal order, and the various retainers bowed or curtsied to the throne and began making their way out.

"You too, General. I would speak with Massha alone."

Badaxe began to object, but Massha nudged him in the ribs with an elbow, a blow which would have been sufficient to flatten most men, but was barely enough to gain the general's attention. He frowned darkly, then gave a short bow and left with the others.

"So, you're a friend of our lord Magician," I asked after we were finally alone.

"I have that . . . honor, your Majesty," Massha replied cautiously. "I hope he's . . . well?"

"As a matter of fact, he's in considerable trouble right now."

Massha heaved a great sigh.

"I was afraid of that. Something to do with his last assignment?"

I ignored the question.

"General Badaxe seems quite taken with you. Are you sure you want to stay in the magik biz? Or are you going to try your hand at a new lifestyle?"

Massha scowled at me.

"Now how did you hear that? You haven't been torturing your own magician, have you?"

I caught the small motion of her adjusting her rings, and decided the time for games was over.

"Hold it, Massha! Before you do anything, there's something I have to show you."

"What's that?"

I had already closed my eyes to remove my disguise spell . . . faster than I ever had before.

"Me," I said, opening my eyes again.

"Well, I'll be . . . you really had me going there, hot stuff."

"It was just a disguise spell," I waved off-handedly.

"Nice. Of course, it almost got you fried. Why didn't you let me know it was you?"

"First of all, I wanted to see if my disguise spell was good enough to fool someone who was watching for it. This is my first time to try to disguise my voice as well as my appearance. Secondly . . . well, I was curious if you had changed your mind about being my apprentice."

"But why couldn't you have just asked me . . . I see.

You're really in trouble, aren't you? Bad enough that you didn't want to drag me into an old promise. That's nice of you, Skeeve. Like I said before, you run a class act."

"Anybody would have done the same thing," I argued, trying to hide my embarrassment at her praise.

She snorted loudly.

"If you believed that, you wouldn't have survived as long as you have. Anyway, apprentice or not, a friend is a friend. Now out with it. What's happened?"

Sitting on the steps to the throne, I filled her in about the forthcoming wedding and my suspicions about the king's conveniently scheduled vacation. I tried to sound casual and matter-of-fact about it, but towards the end my tone got rather flat.

When I was done, Massha gave a low whistle of sympathy.

"When you big leaguers get in trouble, you don't kid around, do you? Now that you've filled me in, I'll admit I'm a little surprised you're still here."

I grimaced.

"I'm a little slow from time to time, but you only have to lecture me once. If one day without a king is bad for a kingdom, a permanent disappearance could be disastrous. Anyway, what I need right now is someone to track down the real king and get him back here, while I keep bluffing from the throne."

Massha scowled.

"Well, I've got a little trinket that could track him, if you've got something around that he's worn, that is. . . ."

"Are you kidding? You think court magicians dress this way in Possiltum? Everything I'm wearing and two more closetsful in his quarters belong to the king."

". . . But what I can't figure out is why you need me? Where's your usual partner . . . whatsisname . . . Aahz? It seems to me he'd be your first choice for a job like this. Wherever he is, can't you just pop over to that dimension and pull him back for a while?"

Lacking any other option, I decided to resort to the truth, both about Aahz's permanent departure and my own lack of ability to travel the dimensions without a D-Hopper. When I was done, Massha was shaking her head.

"So you're all alone and stranded here and you were *still* going to give me an out instead of pressuring me into helping? Well, you got my help, mister, and you don't have to bribe me with an apprenticeship, either. I'll get your king back for you . . . before that wedding. *Then* we'll talk about apprentices."

I shook my head.

"Right idea, but wrong order. I wasn't going to bribe you with an apprenticeship, Massha. I told you before I don't know much magik, but what I know I'll be glad to teach you . . . whether you find the King or not. I'm not sure that's an apprenticeship, but it's yours if you want it."

She smiled, a smile quite different from her usual vamp act.

"We'll argue about it later. Right now, I've got a king to find."

"Wait a minute! Before you go, you're pretty good with gadgets, right? Well, I've got a D-Hopper in my quarters. I want you to show me two settings: the one for Deva, and the one for Klah. You see, I'm not all *that* noble. If things get too rough or it takes you longer than a week to find the king, I want a little running room. If I'm not here when you get back, you can look for your 'noble' Skeeve at the Yellow Crescent Inn at the Bazaar at Deva.''

Massha snorted.

''You're putting yourself down again, Hot Stuff. You're going to try before you run, which is more than I can say for most in our profession. Besides, whatever you think your motives are, they're deeper than you think. You just asked me to show you two settings. You only need one to run.''

Chapter Six:

"Good information is hard to get. Doing anything with it is even harder!"
—L. SKYWALKER

I HAD long since decided that the main requirement for Royalty or its impersonators was an immunity to boredom. Having already chronicled the true tedious nature of performing so-called "duties of state," I can only add that *waiting* to perform them is even worse.

There was certainly no rush on my part to meet the king's bride-to-be, much less marry her. After word had come that her arrival would be delayed by a full day, however, *and* as the day waxed into late afternoon waiting for her "early morning" reception, I found myself wishing that she would get here so we could meet and get it over with already.

All other royal activity had ground to a halt in an effort to emphasize the importance of Possiltum's greeting their queen-to-be. I hardly thought it was necessary, though, as the citizens decked the street with flowers and lined up three deep in hopes of catching a glimpse of this new celebrity. The wait didn't seem to dampen their spirits, though the flowers wilted only to be periodically replaced by eager hands. If nothing else, this reception was going to put a serious dent in Possiltum's flower crop for awhile. Of course, it might also put a dent in *all* our crops, for the streets remained packed with festive people who showed not the slightest inclination to return to their fields or guild shops when word was passed of each new delay.

"Haven't the citizens anything better to do with their time than stand around the streets throwing flowers at each other?" I snarled, turning from the window. "*Somebody* should be keeping the kingdom during all this foolishness."

As usual, J. R. Grimble took it on himself to soothe me.

"Your Majesty is simply nervous about the pending reception. I trust his wisdom will not allow his edginess to spill over onto his loyal subjects?"

"I was assured when she crossed the border that she would be here this morning. Morning! Ever see the sun set in the morning before?"

"Undoubtedly she was delayed by the condition of the roads," General Badaxe offered. "I have told your Majesty before that our roads are long overdue for repair. In their current state, they hinder the passage of travelers . . . *and* troops should our fair land come under attack."

Grimble bared his teeth.

"And his Majesty has always agreed with *me* that repairing the roads at this time would be far too costly . . . unless the General would be willing to significantly reduce the size of his army that we might use the savings from wages to pay for the road work?"

The General purpled.

"Reduce the size of the army and you'll soon lose that treasury that you guard so closely, Grimble."

"Enough, gentlemen," I said, waving them both to

silence. "As you've both said, we've discussed this subject many times before."

It had been decided that rather than having the King of Possiltum sit and fidget in front of the entire populace, that he should sweat it out in private with his advisors until his bride actually arrived. Royal image and all that. Unfortunately this meant that since morning I had been confined in a small room with J. R. Grimble and Hugh Badaxe for company. Their constant bickering and sniping was sufficient to turn my already dubious mood into something of record foulness.

"Well, while we're waiting, perhaps you can each brief me on your opinions of my future bride and her kingdom."

"But your Majesty, we've done that before. Many times."

"Well, we'll do it again. You're supposed to be my advisors, aren't you? So advise me. General Badaxe, why don't you start?"

Badaxe shrugged.

"The situation is essentially unchanged from our last briefing. Impasse is a small kingdom; tiny really—less than a thousand citizens altogether. They claim the entire Impasse mountain range, from which the kingdom gets its name, and which is the bulk of their military defense. Their claim stands mostly because the mountains are treacherous and there is little or no reason to venture there. At least ninety-five percent of their population is concentrated along the one valley through the mountains. They have no formal military, but rather a militia, which suffices as there are no less than five passes in the main valley where a child with a pile of rocks could hold off an army . . . and they have plenty of rocks. Their main vulnerability is food. The terrain is such that they are unable to support even their small

population, and as they are still at odds with the kingdom at the other end of the valley who originally owned
it, they are forced to buy all their food from us . . . at
prices even a generous man would call exorbitant."

"Supply and demand," Grimble said with a toothy
smile.

"Wait a minute, General," I interrupted. "If I understand this right, Impasse is not a threat to us militarily
because of its size. If anything, it guards our flank
against attack from the pass. Right?"

"Correct."

"Which it is already doing."

"Also correct."

Seeing an opening, I hurried on.

"We can't attack them, but from what you say they
don't have anything we want. So why are we bothering
with this marriage/alliance?"

The General looked pointedly at Grimble.

"Because even though Impasse is people-few and
crop-light, they are sitting on the largest deposit of
precious metal on the continent," The Chancellor of the
Exchequer supplied.

"Precious met . . . oh! You mean gold."

"Precisely. With the alliance, Possiltum will become
the richest kingdom ever."

"That hardly seems like sufficient reason to get married," I mumbled.

"Your Majesty's opinions on the subject are well
known to us," Grimble nodded. "You have expressed
them often and long every time the possibility of this
marriage was broached. I am only glad that you finally
gave your consent when the citizens of Possiltum threat-
ened to revolt if you didn't accept the betrothal offer."

"That was only after you spread the word that such

an alliance would significantly lower taxes, Grimble,'' Badaxe scowled.

"I said it *might* lower taxes,'' the Chancellor corrected innocently. "Can I help it if the common folk jumped to conclusions?''

Now that I had a clearer picture of the situation, I might have mustered a bit of sympathy for the King's predicament, if he hadn't stuck me in it in his stead.

"Enough about Impasse. Now give me your opinions of my bride-to-be.''

There was a brief moment of uncomfortable silence.

"Impasse doesn't have a monarchy,'' Grimble said carefully. "That is, until recently. It was more a tribal state, where the strongest ruled. When the last king died, however, his daughter Hemlock somehow managed to take over and maintain the throne, thereby establishing a royal line of sorts. Exactly how she did it is unclear.''

"Some say that prior to the king's death she managed to gain the . . . loyalty of all the able-bodied fighters in the kingdom, thereby securing her claim from challenge,'' Badaxe supplied.

I held up a restraining hand.

"Gentlemen, what you're telling me are facts. I asked for your *opinions*.''

This time, there was a long uncomfortable silence.

"That good, eh?'' I grimaced.

"Your Majesty must remember,'' Grimble protested, "we are being asked to express our hidden feelings about a woman who will soon be our Queen.''

"Not until the marriage,'' I growled. "Right now, I am your king. Get my drift?''

They got it, and swallowed hard.

"The words 'cold-blooded' and 'ruthless' come to

mind," the general said, "and that's the impression of a man who's made a career of the carnage of war."

"I'm sure the rumors that she murdered her father to gain control of the kingdom are exaggerated," Grimble argued weakly.

". . . But your Majesty would be well advised to insist on seperate sleeping quarters, and even then sleep lightly . . . and armed," the general concluded firmly.

"No difficulty should be encountered with separate quarters," Grimble leered. "It's said Queen Hemlock has the morals of an alley cat."

"Terrific," I sighed.

The Chancellor favored me with a paternal smile.

"Oh, there's no doubt that the entire kingdom, myself included, admires your Majesty for the sacrifices he is willing to make for his people."

The trouble was, only *I* knew who the King was willing to sacrifice!

I studied Grimble's smile through hooded eyes, seeking desperately through my mind for something to disrupt his smug enjoyment of the situation. Suddenly, I found it.

"I've been meaning to ask, does anyone know the current whereabouts of our Court Magician?"

Grimble's smile disappeared like water on a hot skillet.

"He's . . . gone, your Majesty."

"What? Out on another of his madcap adventures?"

The Chancellor averted his eyes.

"No, I mean, he's . . . gone. Tendered his resignation and left."

"Tendered his resignation to whom?" I pressed. "On whose authority has he quit his post during this, my darkest hour?"

"Ahh . . . mine, your Majesty."

"What was that, Grimble? I couldn't quite hear you."

"Mine. I told him he could go."

Grimble was sweating visibly now, which was fine by me. In fact, an idea was beginning to form in my mind.

"Hmm . . . knowing you, Lord Chancellor, I would suspect money is behind the Great Skeeve's sudden departure."

"In a way," Grimble evaded, "you might say that."

"Well, it won't do," I said firmly. "I want him back . . . and before this accursed marriage. What's more, since you approved his departure, I'm holding you personally responsible for his return."

"B-ut your Majesty! I wouldn't know where to start looking. He could be anywhere by now."

"He can't have gone far," Badaxe volunteered casually. "His dragon and unicorn are still in the Royal Stables."

"They are?" the Chancellor blinked.

"Yes," the General smiled, "as you might know if you ever set foot outside your counting house."

"See, Grimble," I said. "The task I set before you should be easy for a man of your resources. Now off with you. The longer you tarry here, the longer it will be before you find our wayward magician."

The Chancellor started to say something, then shrugged and started for the door.

"Oh, Grimble," I called. "Something you might keep in mind. I heard a rumor that the Great Skeeve has recently been disguising himself as me for an occasional prank. Like as not the scamp is parading around somewhere with the royal features on his face. That tidbit alone should help you locate him."

"Thank you, your Majesty," the Chancellor responded glumly, reminded now of the shape-changing abilities of his supposed quarry.

I wasn't sure, but I thought General Badaxe was stifling a laugh somewhere in the depths of his beard as his rival trudged out.

"How about you, General? Do you think your men could assist in passing word of my royal summons to the Great Skeeve?"

"That won't be necessary, your Majesty."

With sudden seriousness he approached me, laid a hand on my shoulder, and stared into my eyes.

"Lord Magician," he said, "the King would like to see you."

Chapter Seven:

*"There is no counter for a spirited woman
except spirited drink."*

—R. BUTLER

"YOU'VE known for some time that I'm a fighting man.
What you *don't* seem to realize is what that implies."

We were sitting over wine now, in a much more relaxed conversation than when I had been pretending to
be King Rodrick.

"Fighting men recognize people as much by movement and mannerism as they do by facial feature. It's a
professional habit. Now, you had the appearance and
voice of the King, but your carriage and gestures were
that of the Great Skeeve, not Rodrick the Fifth."

"But if you knew I was an imposter, why didn't you
say something?"

The General drew himself up stiffly.

"The King had not taken me into his confidence in
this matter, nor had you. I felt it would have been rude
to intrude on your affairs uninvited."

"Weren't you afraid that I might be a part of some
plot to murder the King and take his place?"

"Lord Magician, though we met as rivals, prolonged
exposure to you has caused my respect for you to grow

to no small matter. Both in your convincing Big Julie and his army to defect from the Mob and join Possiltum as honest citizens, and in fighting at your side in the Big Game when you risked life and limb to rescue a comrade in peril, you have shown ingenuity, courage, and honor. While I may still speak of you from time to time in less than glowing terms, my lowest opinion of you does not include the possibility of your having a hand in murdering your employer."

"Thank you, General."

". . . And besides, only a total idiot would want to assume Rodrick's place so soon before his marriage to Queen Hemlock."

I winced.

"So much for your growing respect."

"I said 'ingenuity, courage, and honor.' I made no mention of intelligence. Very well, then, a total idiot or someone under orders from his king."

"How about a bit of both?" I sighed.

"I suspected as much." Badaxe nodded. "Now that we're speaking candidly, may I ask as to the whereabouts of the King?"

"Good question."

In a few depressing sentences, I brought him up to date on my assignment and Rodrick's disappearance.

"I was afraid something like this would happen," the General said when I concluded. "The King has been looking desperately for some way out of this marriage, and it looks like he's found it. Well, needless to say, if there's anything I can do to help, just ask."

"Thanks, General. As a matter of fact, I. . . ."

". . . As long as it doesn't go against the good of the kingdom," Badaxe amended. "Like helping you to escape. Possiltum needs a king, and for the time being, you're it!"

"Oh. Well . . . how about using your men to help find the king?"

Badaxe shook his head.

"Can't do it. Massha has that assignment. If I sent my men to back her up, she'd think I didn't have any faith in her."

Terrific! I had an ally, if I could get around his loyalties and amorous entanglements.

The General must have noticed my expression.

"Anything else I'll be willing to do."

"Like what?"

"Well . . . like teaching you to defend yourself against your bride-to-be."

That actually sounded promising.

"Do you think we'll have enough time?"

With that, there was a heavy knocking at the door.

"Your Majesty! The carriage of Queen Hemlock is approaching the palace!"

"No," said the General, with disheartening honesty.

We barely made it to our appointed places ahead of the Queen's procession. The throne of Possiltum had been temporarily moved to a position just inside the doors to the palace, and only by sprinting through the corridors with undignified abandon were Badaxe and I able to reach our respective positions before the portals were thrown open.

"Remind me to have a word with you about the efficiency of your army's early warning system," I said to the General as I sank into my seat.

"I believe it was the Court Magician who complained about the excessive range of the military spy system," Badaxe retorted. "Perhaps your Majesty will see fit now to convince him of the necessity of timely information."

Before I could think of a sufficiently polite response,

the Queen's party drew to a halt at the foot of the stairs.

The kingdom of Impasse had apparently spared no expense on the Queen's carriage. If it was not actually fashioned of solid gold, there were sufficient quantities of the metal in the trim and decorations as to make the difference academic. I took secret pleasure that Grimble was not present to gloat at the scene. The curtains were drawn, allowing us to see the rich embroidery upon them, but not who or what was within. A team of eight matched horses completed the rig, though their shaggy coats and short stature suggested that normally the mountainfolk put them to far more practical use than dragging royalty around the countryside.

With the carriage, however, any semblance of decorum about the Queen's procession vanished.

Her escort consisted of at least twenty retainers, all mounted and leading extra horses, though whether these were relief mounts or the bride's dowry I couldn't tell. The escort was also all male, and of a uniform appearance; broad-shouldered, narrow-waisted, and musclebound. They reminded me of miniature versions of the opposing teams Aahz and I had faced during the Big Game, but unlike those players, these men were armed to the teeth. They fairly bristled with swords and knives, glittering from boot-tops, arm sheaths, and shoulder scabbards, such that I was sure the combined weight of their weapons offset that of the golden coach they were guarding. These weren't pretty court decorations, but well handled field weapons worn with the ease fighting men accord the tools of their trade.

The men themselves were dressed in drab tunics suited more for crawling through thickets with knives clenched in their teeth than serving as a royal escort. Still, they wrinkled their broad, flat features into wide smiles as they alternately gawked at the building and waved at the

crowd which seemed determined to unload the earlier
noted surplus of flowers by burying the coach with
them. The escort may have seemed sloppy and un-
disciplined in the eyes of Badaxe or Big Julie, but I
wouldn't want to be the one to try to take anything
away from them; Queen, coach, kingdom, or even a
flower they had taken a fancy to.

Two men in the procession were notable exceptions to
the rule. Even on horseback they looked to be head and
shoulder taller than the others and half again as broad.
They had crammed their massive frames into tunics
which were clean and formal, and appeared to be
unarmed. I noted, however, that instead of laughing or
waving, they sat ramrod stiff in their saddles and
surveyed their surroundings with the bored, detached
attention to detail I normally associated with predators . . . big predators.

I was about to call Badaxe's attention to the pair
when the carriage door opened. The woman who appeared was obviously akin to most of the men in the
escort. She had the same broad, solid build and facial
features, only more so. My first impression was that she
looked like the bottom two-thirds of an oak door, if the
door were made of granite. Unsmiling, she swept the
area with a withering stare, then nodded to herself and
stepped down.

"Lady in waiting," Badaxe murmured.

I'm not sure if his comment was meant to reassure
me, but it did. Only after did it occur to me that the
General had volunteered the information to keep me
from running, which I had been seriously considering.

The next figure in view was a radical departure from
the other Impassers in the party. She was arrow thin and
pale with black stringy black hair that hung straight past
her shoulders. Instead of the now expected round, flat

face, her features looked like she had been hung up by
her nose to dry. She wasn't unpleasant to look at, in
fact, I guessed that she was younger than I was, but the
pointed nose combined with a pair of dark, shiny-alert
eyes gave her a vaguely rodent appearance. Her dress
was a long-sleeved white thing that would have probably
looked more fetching on a clothes-hanger. Without
more than a glance at the assembled citizens she
gathered up what slack there was in the skirt, hopped
down from the carriage, and started up the stairs toward
me with the athletic, leggy grace of a confirmed tom-
boy.

"*That* is Queen Hemlock," the General supplied.

I had somehow suspected as much, but having received confirmation, I sprang into action. *This* part, at
least, I knew how to handle, having had it drilled into
me over and over again by my advisors.

I rose to my feet and stood regally until she reached
the throne, then timed my bow to coincide with her curtsey . . . monarch greeting monarch and all that.

Next, I was supposed to welcome her to Possiltum,
but before I could get my mouth open, she came up with
her own greeting.

"Sorry I didn't curtsey any lower, but I'm not wearing a thing under this dress. Rod, it's beastly hot here in
the lowlands," she said, giving me a wide but thin-
lipped smile.

"Aahh. .. .." I said carefully.

Ignoring my response, or lack thereof, she smiled and
waved at the throng, which responded with a roar of approval.

"What idiot invited the rabble?" she asked, the smile
never leaving her face.

"Aahh. . . ." I repeated.

General Badaxe came to my rescue.

"No formal announcement was made, your Majesty, but word of your arrival seems to have leaked out to the general populace. As might be expected, they are very eager to see their new Queen."

"Looking like this?" she said, baring her teeth and waving to those on the rooftops. "Six days on the road in this heat without a bath or a change of clothes and instead of a discreet welcome, half the kingdom gets to see me looking like I was dragged along behind the coach instead of riding in it. Well, it's done and we can't change it. But mind you, if it happens again . . . General Badaxe, is it? I thought so. Anyway, as I was saying, if it happens again, heads will roll . . . and I'm not speaking figuratively."

"Welcome to Possiltum," I managed at last.

It was a considerably abbreviated version of the speech I had planned to give, but it was as much as I could remember under the circumstances.

"Hello, Roddie," she said without looking at me, still waving at the crowd. "I'm going to scamper off for my quarters in a second. Be a love and try not to get underfoot during the next week . . . there's so much to do. Besides, it looks like you're going to have your hands full with other business."

"How's that?"

"You've got a wee bit of trouble coming your way, at least, according to the gentleman I met on the road. Here he comes now. Bye."

"But . . ."

Queen Hemlock had already disappeared, vanishing into the depths of the palace like a puff of smoke. Instead, I found myself focusing on the man who had stepped from the carriage and was currently trudging up the stairs toward my throne. I observed that he had the same weasel features and manners of J. R. Grimble.

Mostly, though, I noticed that the two broadshouldered predators previously assumed to be part of the Queen's escort, had suddenly materalized at his side, towering over him like a pair of bookends . . . mean looking bookends.

I sat down, in part because the approaching figure did not seem to be royalty, but mostly because I had a feeling I wanted to be sitting down for this next interview.

The man reached my throne at last, drew himself up, and gave a curt nod rather than a bow. This, at least, looked polite, since his flankers didn't acknowledge my presence at all.

"Forgive me for intruding on such a festive occasion, your Majesty," the man said, "but there are certain matters we need to discuss."

"Such as . . . ?"

"My name is Shai-ster, and I represent a . . . consortium of businessmen. I wish to confer with one of your retainers concerning certain employees of ours who failed to report in after pursuing our interests in this region."

As I mentioned earlier, I was getting pretty good at speaking "bureaucrat." This man's oration, however, lost me completely.

"You want to what about who?"

The man sighed and hung his head for a moment.

"Let me put it to you this way," he said at last. "I'm with the Mob, and I want to see your Magician, Skeeve. It's about our army, Big Julie's boys, that sort of disappeared after tangling with him. Now do you understand me?"

Chapter Eight:

*"Choose your friends carefully. Your ene-
mies will choose you!"*

—Y. ARAFAT

WITHIN a few days of Queen Hemlock's arrival, the
palace of Possiltum had the happy, relaxed air of a bat-
tlefield the night before the battle. The Queen's party
and the mob representatives were housed in the palace
as "royal guests," giving me a two-front war whether I
wanted it or not.

Queen Hemlock was not an immediate problem; she
was more like a time bomb. With specific orders to
"stay out of her way," I didn't have to deal with her
much, and even General Badaxe admitted that if she
were going to try to kill me, it wouldn't be until after the
wedding when she was officially Queen of Possiltum.
Still, as the wedding day loomed closer, I was increas-
ingly aware that she would have to be dealt with.

The Mob representatives, however, were an immediate problem. I had stalled them temporarily by telling them that the Court Magician was not currently in
the palace, but had been sent for, and as a token of
good faith had given them the hospitality of the palace.
They didn't drink much, and never pestered me with

questions about "Skeeve's" return. There was no doubt in my mind, however, that at some time their patience would be exhausted and they would start looking for the Court Magician themselves. I also had a felling that "some time" would be real soon.

Needing all the help I could get, I had Badaxe send one of his men for Big Julie. With minimal difficulty we smuggled him into the palace, and the three of us held a war council. On Badaxe's advice, I immediately dropped my disguise and brought our guest up to date on the situation.

"Ah'm sorry," Julie said to open the meeting, "but I don't see where I can help you, know what I mean?"

Terrific. So much for Big Julie's expert military advice.

"I'd *like* to help," he clarified. "You've done pretty good by me and the boys. But I used to work for the Mob, you know? I know what they're like. Once they get on your trail, they never quit. I tried to tell you that before."

"I don't see what the problem is," General Badaxe rumbled. "There are only three of them, and their main spokesman's a non-combatant to boot. It wouldn't take much to make sure they didn't report anything to anybody . . . ever again."

Big Julie shook his head.

"You're a good man, Hugh, but you don't know what you're dealing with here. If the Mob's scouting party disappears, the Big Boys will know they've hit paydirt and set things in motion. Taking out their reps won't stop the Mob . . . it won't even delay them. If anything, it will speed the process up!"

Before Badaxe had a chance to reply, I interrupted with a few questions of my own.

"Wait a minute, Big Julie. When we first met, you

were commanding the biggest army this world had ever seen. Right?"

"That's right," he nodded. "We was rolling along pretty good until we met you."

". . . And we didn't stop you militarily. We just gave you a chance to disappear as soldiers and retire as citizens of Possiltum. You and your boys were never beaten in a fight."

"We were the best," Big Julie confirmed proudly. "Anybody messed with us, they pulled back a bloody stump with no body attached, know what I mean?"

"Then why are you all so afraid of the Mob? If they try anything, why don't you and your boys just hook up with General Badaxe's army and teach 'em a lesson in maneuvers?"

The ex-commander heaved a deep sigh.

"It don't work that way," he said. "If they was to march in here like an army, sure, we could send 'em packing. But they won't. They move in a few muscle-men at a time, all acting just as polite as you please so there's nothing you can arrest 'em for. When enough of 'em get here, though, they start leaning on your citizens. Little stuff, but nasty. If somebody complains to you, that somebody turns up dead along with most of their family. Pretty soon, all your citizens are more afraid of the Mob than they are of you. Nobody complains, nobody testifies in court. When that happens, you got no more kingdom. The Mob runs everything while you starve. You can't fight an invasion like that with an army. You can't fight it at all!"

We all sat in uncomfortable silence for a while, each avoiding the other's gaze while we racked our brains for a solution.

"What I don't understand," Badaxe said at last, "is if the system you describe is so effective and so unstoppable, why did they bother having an army at all?"

"I really hate to admit this," Big Julie grimaced, "but we was an experiment. Some of the Mob's bean-counters got it into their heads that even though an army was more expensive, the time savings of a fast takeover would offset the additional cost. To tell you the truth, I think their experiment was a washout."

That one threw me.

"You mean to say your army wasn't effective?"

"Up to a point we were. After that, we were too big. It costs a lot to keep an army in the field, and toward the end there, it was costing more to support my boys for a week than we were getting out of the kingdoms we were conquering. I think they were getting ready to phase us out . . . and that's why it's taken so long for them to come looking for their army."

I shook my head quickly.

"You lost me on that last loop, Big Julie. *Why* did they delay their search?"

"Money," he said firmly. "I'll tell you, nothing makes the Big Boys sit up and take notice like hard cash. I mean, they wrote the book when it came to money motivation."

"Sounds like Grimble," Badaxe muttered. "Doesn't anybody do anything for plain old revenge anymore?"

"Stow it, General," I ordered, leaning forward. "Keep going, Big Julie. What part does money have in this?"

"Well, the way I see it, the Mob was already losing money on my army, you know? To me, that means they weren't about to throw good gold after bad. I mean, why spend more money looking for an army that, when you find it, is only going to cost you more money?"

"But they're here now."

"Right. At the same time Possiltum's about to

become suddenly rich. It looks to me like the Big Boys have found a way to settle a few old scores and turn a profit at the same time."

"The wedding!" I said. "I should have known. That means that by calling off the wedding, I can eliminate two problems at once; Queen Hemlock, *and* the Mob!"

Badaxe scowled at me.

"I thought we had already discarded that option. Remember Grimble and the citizenry of Possiltum?"

Without thinking, I slammed the flat of my hand down on the table with a loud slap.

"Will you forget about Grimble and the citizenry of Possiltum? I'm tired of being in a box, General, and one way or another I'm going to blast a way out!"

From the expressions of my advisors, I realized I might have spoken louder than I had intended. With a conscious effort, I modulated my tone and my mood.

"Look, General . . . Hugh," I said carefully. "You may be used to the pressures of command, but this is new to me. I'm a magician, remember? Forgive me if I get a little razzled trying to find a solution to the problem that your . . . I mean, *our* King has dropped in my lap. Okay?"

He nodded curtly, but still didn't relax.

"Now, your point has merit," I continued, "but it overlooks a few things. First, Grimble isn't here. When and *if* he does get back, he'll have the king in tow, and friend Rodrick can solve the problem for us . . . at least the problem with the Queen. As for the citizenry of Possiltum . . . between you and me I'm almost ready to face their protests rather than have to deal with Queen Hemlock. Now if you weigh the disappointment of our people over having to continue the status quo against having both the Queen *and* the Mob move in on a permanent basis, what result do you get? Thinking of the welfare of the kingdom, of course!"

The General thought it over, then heaved a great sigh.

"I was never that much in favor of the wedding, anyway," he admitted.

"Just a minute, boys," Big Julie said, holding up a weary hand. "It's not quite that easy. The money thing may have slowed up their search a bit, but now that the Mob is here, there are a couple other matters they're gonna want to settle."

"Such as?" I asked, dreading the answer.

"Well, first off, there's me and my boys. Nobody just walks away from the Mob, you know. Their pay scale is great, but their retirement plan stinks."

"I thought you said they didn't want their army anymore," Badaxe grumbled.

"Maybe not as an army, but they can always use manpower. They'll probably break us up and absorb us into various positions in the organization."

"Would you be willing to go back to work for them?"

Big Julie rubbed his chin with one hand as he considered the General's question.

"I'd have to talk to the boys," he said. "Like I said, this kingdom's been pretty good to us. I'd hate to see anything happen to it because we were here . . . especially if we'd end up working for them again anyway."

"No," I said flatly.

"But . . ."

"I said 'No!' You've got a deal with Possiltum, Big Julie. More important, you've got a deal with me. We don't turn you over to the Mob until we've tried everything we can do to defend you."

"And how do you propose to defend them from the Mob?" Badaxe asked, sarcastically.

"I don't know. I'm working on it. Maybe we can buy

them off. Offer them Queen Hemlock to hold for ransom or something."

"Lord Magician!"

"Okay, okay. I said I was still working on it, didn't I? What's next, Big Julie? You said there were a couple things they wanted besides money."

"You," he said bluntly. "The Mob isn't going to be happy until they get the Great Skeeve, Court Magician of Possiltum."

"Me?" I said in a small voice.

"The Mob didn't get to the top by ignoring the competition. You've made some pretty big ripples with your work, and the biggest as far as they're concerned is making their army disappear. They know you're big. Big enough to be a threat. They're gonna want you neutralized. My guess is that they'll try to hire you, and failing that, try for some sort of non-aggression deal."

"And failing that . . . ?" Badaxe asked, echoing my thoughts.

Big Julie shrugged.

"Failing that, they're gonna do their best to kill you."

Chapter Nine:

"I don't know why anyone would be nervous about going to see royalty."

—P. IN BOOTS

"BUT why do *I* have to come along?" Badaxe protested, pacing along at my side as we strode towards the Queen's chambers.

"Call it moral support," I growled. "Besides, I want a witness that I went into the Queen's chambers . . . and came out again, if you get my drift."

"But if this will only solve one of our problems. . . ."

". . . Then it will be one less problem for us to deal with. Shh! Here we are."

I had switched back to my Rodrick disguise. That combined with the General's presence was enough to have the Honor Guards at the Queen's chambers snap to rigid attention at our approach. I ignored them and hammered on the door, though I did have a moment to reflect that not long ago, I thought the biggest problem facing a king was boredom!

"For cryin' out loud!" came a shrill voice from within. "Can't you guards get *anything* right? I told you I didn't want to be disturbed!"

One of the guards rolled his eyes in exasperation. I

favored him with a sympathetic smile, then raised an eyebrow at Badaxe.

"King Rodrick the Fifth of Possiltum seeks an audience with Queen Hemlock!" he bellowed.

"I suppose it's all right," came the reply. "How about first thing in the morning?"

"Now," I said.

I didn't say it very loud, but it must have carried. Within a few heartbeats the door flew open, exposing Queen Hemlock . . . literally. I can't describe her clothing because she wasn't wearing any. Not a stitch!

"Roddie!" she chirped, oblivious to the guards and Badaxe, all of whom gaped at her nakedness. "Come on in. What in the world are you doing here?"

"Wait for me," I instructed Badaxe in my most commanding tone.

"C-certainly, your Majesty!" he responded, tearing his eyes away from the Queen long enough to snap to attention.

With that, I stepped into the Queen's lair.

"So, what have you got for me?" She shut the door and leaned back against it. The action made her point at me, even though her hands were behind her back.

"I beg your pardon?"

"The audience," she clarified. "You wanted it, you got it. What's up?"

Somehow under the circumstances, I found that to be another embarrassing question.

"I . . . um . . . that is . . . could you please put something on? I'm finding your attire, or lack thereof, to be quite distracting."

"Oh, very well. It *is* beastly hot in here, though."

She flounced across the room and came up with a flimsy something which she shrugged into, but didn't close completely.

"Right after the wedding," she declared, "I want that window enlarged, or better yet, the whole wall torn out. Anything to get a little ventilation in this place."

She plopped down in a chair and curled her legs up under her. It eased my discomfort somewhat, but not much.

"Ahh . . . actually, that's what I'm here to talk to you about."

"The window?" she frowned.

"No. The wedding."

That made her frown even more.

"I thought it was agreed that I would handle all the wedding arrangements. Oh, well, if you've got any specific changes, it isn't too late to. . . ."

"It isn't that," I interrupted hastily. "It's . . . well, it's come to my attention that the high prices Possiltum is charging your kingdom for food is forcing you into this marriage. Not wishing to have you enter into such a bond under duress, I've decided to cut our prices in half, thereby negating the need for our wedding."

"Oh, Roddie, don't be silly. That's not the reason I'm marrying you!"

Rather than being upset, the Queen seemed quite amused at my suggestion.

"It isn't?"

"Of course not. Impasse is so rich that we could buy your yearly crop at double the prices if we wanted to and still not put a dent in our treasury."

My stomach began to sink.

"Then you *really* want this marriage? You aren't being forced into it for political reasons?"

The Queen flashed all her teeth at me in a quick smile.

"Of course there are political reasons. I mean, we are royalty, aren't we? I'm sure you're a pleasant enough fellow, but I can get all the pleasant fellows I want without *marrying* them. Royalty marries power blocks, not people.''

There was a glimmer of hope in what she was saying, and I pounced on it with all fours.

''. . . Which brings us to the other reason we should call off the wedding,'' I said grandly.

The Queen's smile disappeared.

''What's that?'' she said sharply.

For my reply, I let drop my disguise spell.

''Because I'm not Royalty. I'm people.''

''Oh, that,'' the Queen shrugged. ''No problem. I knew that all along.''

''You did?'' I gulped.

''Sure. You were embarrassed . . . twice. Once when I arrived at the palace, and again just now when I opened the door in my all-together. Royalty doesn't embarrass. It's in the blood. I knew all long you weren't Rodrick. It's my guess you're the Great Skeeve, Court Magician. Right? The one who can shape change?''

''Well, it's a disguise spell, not shape changing, but except for that, you're right.''

Between Badaxe and Queen Hemlock, I was starting to wonder if anyone was really fooled by my disguise spells.

The Queen uncoiled from her seat and began pacing back and forth as she spoke, oblivious to her nakedness which peeked out of her wrap at each turn.

''The fact that you aren't the king doesn't change my situation, if anything it improves it. As long as you can keep your disguise up enough to fool the rabble, I'll be marrying two power blocks instead of one.''

''Two power blocks,'' I echoed hollowly.

''Yes. As the 'king' of Possiltum, you control the first block I was after: land and people. Impasse by itself isn't large enough to wage an aggressive war, but uniting the respective powers of the two kingdoms, we're unstoppable. With your armies backed by my capital, I can sweep as far as I want, which is pretty far, let me tell you. There's nothing like growing up in a valley where the only view is the other side of the valley to whet one's appetite for new and unusual places.''

"Most people content themselves with touring," I suggested. "You don't have to conquer a country to see it.''

"Cute,'' Queen Hemlock sneered. "Naive, but cute. Let's just say I'm not most people and let it ride, okay? Now then, for the second power base, there's you and your magic. That's a bonus I hadn't expected, but I'm sure that, given a day or two, I can expand my plans to take advantage of it.''

At one time, I thought I had been scared by Massha. In hindsight, Massha caused me only faint discomfort. Talking with Queen Hemlock, I learned what fear was all about! She wasn't just a murderess, as Badaxe suspected. She was utter mayhem waiting to be loosed on the world. The only thing between her and the resources necessary to act out her dreams was me. Me, and maybe. . . .

"What about King Rodrick?" I blurted out. "If he shows up, the original wedding plans go into effect.''

"You mean he's still alive?" she exclaimed, arching a thin eyebrow at me. "I've overestimated you, Skeeve. Alive he could be a problem. No matter. I'll alert my escort to kill him on sight if he appears before the wedding. After we're married, it would be a simple matter to declare him an imposter and have him officially executed.''

Terrific. Thanks to my big mouth, Massha would be walking into a trap if she tried to return the King to the castle. If Queen Hemlock's men saw him, then . . .

"Wait a minute!" I exclaimed. "If I'm walking around disguised as the King, what's to keep your men from offing me by mistake?"

"Hmm. Good thing you thought about that. Okay! Here's what we'll do."

She dove into her wardrobe and emerged with a length of purple ribbon.

"Wear this in full view whenever you're outside your chambers," she instructed, thrusting it into my hands. "It'll let my men know that you're the man I want to marry instead of their target."

I stood with the ribbon in my hand.

"Aren't you making a rather large assumption, your Majesty?"

"What's that?" she frowned.

"That I may not want to marry you?"

"Of course you do," she smiled. "You've already got the throne of Possiltum. If you marry me, you not only have access to my treasury, it also rids you of your other problem."

"My other problem?"

"The Mob, silly. Remember? I rode in with their representative. With my money, you can buy them off. They'll forget anything if the price is high enough. Now, isn't being my husband better than running from their vengeance *and* mine for the rest of your life?"

I had my answer to that, but in a flash of wisdom kept it to myself. Instead, I said my goodbyes and left.

"From your expression, I take it that your interview with the Queen was less than a roaring success," Badaxe said dryly.

"Spare me the 'I told you so's,' General," I snarled. "We've got work to do."

Shooting a quick glance up and down the corridor, I cut my purple ribbon in half on the edge of his axe.

"Keep a lookout for Massha and the King," I instructed. "If you see them, be sure Rodrick wears this. It'll make his trip through the palace a lot easier."

"But where are you going?"

I gave him a tight smile.

"To see the Mob representatives. Queen Hemlock has graciously told me how to deal with them!"

Chapter Ten:

"Superior firepower is an invaluable tool when entering into negotiations."

—G. PATTON

THE Mob representatives had been housed in one of the less frequented corners of the palace. In theory, this kept them far from the hub of activity while Badaxe and I figured out what to do with them. In fact, it meant that now that I was ready to face them, I had an awfully long walk to reach my destination.

By the time I reached the proper door, I was so winded I wasn't sure I'd have enough breath to announce my presence. Still, on my walk I had worked up a bit of a mad against the Mob. I mean, who did they think they were, popping up and disrupting my life this way? Besides, I was too unnerved by Queen Hemlock to try anything against her, which left the Mob as the only target for my frustration.

With that in mind, I drew a deep breath and knocked on the door.

I needn't have worried about announcing myself. Between the second and third knocks, the door opened a crack. My third knock hit the door before I could stop it, but the door remained unmoved by the impact.

71

"Hey, Shai-ster! It's the King!"

"Well, let him in, you idiot!"

The door opened wide, revealing one of Shai-ster's massive bodyguards, then a little wider to allow me entry space past him.

"Come in, come in, your Majesty," the Mob's spokesman said, hurrying forward to greet me. "Have a drink . . . Dummy! Get the King something to drink!"

This last was addressed to the second hulking muscleman who heaved himself off the bed he had been sprawled upon. With self-conscious dignity he picked up the end of the bed one-handed, set it down again, then picked up the mattress and extracted a small, flat bottle from under it.

I wondered briefly if this was what Big Julie meant when he referred to the Mob tradition of "going to the mattresses." Somehow the phrase had always brought another image to mind . . . something involving women.

Accepting the flask from his bodyguard, Shai-ster opened the top and offered it to me, smiling all the while.

"Am I correct in assuming that your Majesty's visit indicates news of the whereabouts of his court magician? Perhaps even an estimated time as to when he is expected back?"

I accepted the flask, covertly checking the locations of the bodyguards before I answered. One was leaning against the door, while the other stood by the bed.

"Actually, I can do better than that. The Great Skeeve . . ."

I closed my eyes and dropped my disguise spell.

". . . is here."

The bodyguards started visibly at my transformation, but Shai-ster remained unmoved except for a narrowing of the eyes and a tightening of his smile.

"I see. That simplifies things a bit. Boys, give the Great Skeeve here a chair. We have some business to discuss."

His tone was not pleasant, nor were the bodyguards smiling as they started for me.

Remember how Rupert jumped me so easily? Well, he took me by surprise, and had three hundred years plus of magical practice to boot. Somehow, I was not particularly surprised by the bodyguards' action . . . in fact, I had been expecting it and had been gathering my powers for just this moment.

With a theatric wave of my hand and a much more important focusing of my mental energies, I picked the two men up and spun them in midair. Heck, I wasn't adverse to stealing a new idea for how to use levitation . . . even from Rupert. I did like a little originality in my work, though, so instead of bouncing them on their heads, I slammed them against the ceiling and held them pinned there.

"No, thanks," I said as casually as I could, "I'd rather stand."

Shai-ster looked at his helpless protectors, then shot a hard stare at me.

"Perhaps this won't be as simple as I thought," he admitted. "Say, you've got a unicorn, don't you?"

"That's right," I confirmed, surprised by the sudden change in topic.

"I don't suppose you'd be particularly scared if you woke up in the morning and found him in your bed . . . not all of him, just his head?"

"Scared? No, not particularly. In fact, I'm pretty sure I'd be mad enough to quit playing games and get down to serious revenge."

The Mob spokesman sighed heavily.

"Well, that's that. If we can't make a deal, we'll just

have to do this the hard way. You can let the boys down now. We'll be heading back in the morning.''

This time, it was my turn to smile.

''Not so fast. Who said I didn't want to make a deal?''

For the first time since I met him, Shai-ster's poise was shaken.

''But . . . I thought . . . if you can . . .''

''Don't assume, Shai-ster. It's a bad habit for businessmen to get into. I just don't like to get pushed around, that's all. Now then, as you said earlier, I believe we have some business to discuss.''

The spokesman shot a nervous glance at the ceiling.

''Um . . . could you let the boys down first? It's a bit distracting.''

''Sure.''

I closed my eyes and released the spell. Mind you, unlike the disguise spell, I don't have to close my eyes to remove a levitation spell. I just didn't want to see the results.

The room shook as two loud crashes echoed each other. I distinctly heard the bed assume a foolproof disguise as kindling.

I carefully opened an eye.

One bodyguard was unconscious. The other rolled about, groaning weakly.

''They're down,'' I said, needlessly.

Shai-ster ignored me.

''Big bad bodyguards! Wait'll the Big Boys hear how good dumb muscle is against magik!''

He paused to kick the groaner in the side.

''Groan quieter! *Mister* Skeeve and I have some talking to do.''

Having already completed one adventure after antagonizing the military arm of a large organization, I was not overly eager to add another entire group of plug-uglies to my growing list of enemies.

"Nothing personal," I called to the bodyguard who was still conscious. "Here! Have a drink."

I levitated the flask over to him, and he caught it with a weak moan I chose to interpret as "thanks."

"You said something about a deal?" Shai-ster said, turning to me again.

"Right. Now, if my appraisal of the situation is correct, the Mob wants three things: Big Julie's army back, me dead or working for them, and a crack at the new money coming into Possiltum after the wedding."

The Mob spokesman cocked his head to one side.

"That's a bit more blunt than I would have put it, but you appear to have captured the essential spirit of my clients' wishes. My compliments on your concise summation."

"Here's another concise summation to go with it. Hands off Big Julie and his crew; he's under my protection. By the same token, Possiltum is my territory. Stay away from it or it will cost you more than you'll get. As to my services, I have no wish to become a Mob employee. I would consider an occasional assignment as an outside contractor for a specific fee, but full-time employment is out."

The Mob spokesman was back in his element, face stony and impassive.

"That doesn't sound like much of a deal."

"It doesn't?"

I reviewed the terms quickly in my mind.

"Oh! Excuse me. There is one other important part of my offer I neglected to mention. I don't expect your employers to give up their objectives without any return at all. What I have in mind is a swap: an army and maybe a kingdom for an opportunity to exploit an entire world.''

Shai-ster raised his eyebrows.

''You're going to give us the world? Just like that? Lord Magician, I suspect you're not bargaining with a full deck.''

''I didn't say I would give you the world, I said I would give you *access* to a world. Brand new territory full of businesses and people to exploit; one of the richest in the universe.''

The spokesman frowned.

''Another world? And I'm supposed to take your word as to how rich it is and that you can give us access?''

''It would be nice, but even in my most naive moments I wouldn't expect you to accept a blind bid like that. No, I'm ready to give you a brief tour of the proposed world so that you can judge for yourself.''

''Wait a minute,'' Shai-ster said, holding up his hands. ''This is so far beyond my negotiating parameters that even if I liked what I saw, I couldn't approve the deal. I need to bring one of the Big Boys in on this decision.''

This was better than I had hoped. By the time he could bring one of the Mob's hierarchy to Possiltum, I could deal with some of my other problems.

''Fine. Go and fetch him. I'll hold the deal until your return.''

The spokesman gave one of his tight-lipped smiles.

''No need to wait,'' he said. ''My immediate superior is on call specifically for emergencies such as this.''

Before I could frame a reply, he opened the front of his belt-buckle and began rubbing it, all the while mumbling under his breath.

There was a quick flash of light, and an old, hairy-jowled man appeared in the room. Looking round, he spied the two bodyguards sprawled on the floor and gripped the sides of his face with his open hands in an exaggerated expression of horror.

"Mercy!" he wheezed in a voice so hoarse I could barely understand him. "Shai-ster, you bad boy. If there was trouble, you should have called me sooner. Oh, those poor, poor boys."

The Mob spokesman's face was once again blank and impassive as he addressed me.

"Skeeve, Lord Magician of Possiltum, let me introduce Don Bruce, the Mob's fairy godfather."

Chapter Eleven:

*"Tell you what. Let me sweeten the deal a
bit for you. . . . "*

—BEELZEBUB

"OH! This is simply *mar*-velous! Who would have ever
thought . . . another dimension, you say?"

"That's right," I said off-handedly. "It's called
Deva."

Of course, I was quite in agreement with Don Bruce.
The Bazaar on Deva was really something, and every
time I visited it, I was impressed anew. It was an incredible tangle of tents and displays stretching as far as the
eye could see in every direction, crammed full of enough
magikal devices and beings to defy anyone's imagina-
tion and sanity. It was the main crossroads of trade for
the dimensions. Anything worth trading money or
credits for was here.

This time, however, I was the senior member of the
expedition. As much as I wanted to rubberneck and ex-
plore, it was more important to pretend to be bored and
worldly . . . or other-worldly as the case might be.

Don Bruce led the parade, as wide-eyed as a farm-kid
in his first big city, with Shai-ster, myself, and the two

bodyguards trailing along behind. The bodyguards seemed more interested in crowding close to me than in protecting their superiors, but then again, they had just had some bad experiences with magik.

"The people here all look kinda strange," one of them muttered to me. "You know, like foreigners."

"They are foreigners . . . or rather *you* are," I said. "You're on their turf, and a long way from home. These are Deveels."

"Devils?" the man responded, looking a little wild-eyed. "You're tellin' me we're surrounded by devils?"

While it was reassuring to me to see the Mob's bully-boys terrified by something I had grown used to, it also occurred to me that if they were *too* scared, it might ruin the deal I was trying to set up.

"Look . . . say, what is your name, anyway?"

"Guido," the man confided, "and this here's my cousin Nunzio."

"Well look, Guido. Don't be thrown by these jokers. Look at them. They're storekeepers like storekeepers anywhere. Just because they look funny doesn't mean they don't scare like anybody else."

"I suppose you're right. Say, I meant to thank you for the drink back there at the castle."

"Don't mention it," I waved. "It was the least I could do after bouncing you off the ceiling. Incidentally, there was nothing personal in that. I wasn't trying to make you two look bad, I was trying to make myself look good . . . if you see the difference."

Guido's brow furrowed slightly.

"I . . . think so. Yeah! I get it. Well, it worked. You looked real good. I wouldn't want to cross you, and neither would Nunzio. In fact, if we can ever do you a favor . . . you know, bend someone a little for you . . . well, just let us know."

"Hey, what's that?"

I looked in the direction Don Bruce was pointing. A booth was filled with short painted sticks, all floating in midair.

"I think he's selling magic wands," I guessed.

"Oh! I want one. Now, don't go anywhere without me."

The bodyguards hesitated for a moment, then followed as Don Bruce plunged into negotiations with the booth's proprietor, who gaped a bit at his new customer.

"Does he always dress like that?" I asked Shai-ster. "You know, all in light purple?"

The Mob spokesman raised an eyebrow at me.

"Do you always dress in green when you travel to other dimensions?"

Just to be on the safe side, I had donned another disguise before accompanying this crew to Deva. It occurred to me that if I were successful in my negotiations, it wouldn't be wise to be known at the Bazaar as the one who introduced organized crime to the dimension.

Unfortunately, this had dawned on me just as we were preparing to make our departure, so I hadn't had much time to choose someone to disguise myself as. Any of my friends were out, as were Massha, Quigley, Garkin . . . in desperation I settled on Rupert . . . I mean, there was one being I owed a bad turn or two. Consequently, I was currently parading around the Bazaar as a scaly green Pervert . . . excuse me, Pervect.

"I have my reasons," I dodged loftily.

"Well, so has Don Bruce," Shai-ster scowled. "Now if you don't mind, I've got a few questions about this place. If we try to move in here, won't language be a problem? I can't understand anything these freaks are saying."

"Take a look," I instructed, pointing.

Don Bruce and the Deveel proprietor were haggling earnestly, obviously having no difficulty understanding each other, however much they disagreed.

"No Deveel worth his salt is going to let a little thing like language stand in the way of a sale."

"Hey, everybody! Look what I got!"

We turned to find Don Bruce bearing down on us, proudly waving a small rod the same color as his clothes.

"It's a magic wand!" he exclaimed. "I got it for a song."

"A song plus some gold, I'd wager," Shai-ster observed dryly. "What does it do?"

"What does it do?" Don Bruce grinned. "Watch this."

He swept the wand across the air with a grand gesture, and a cloud of shiny dust sparkled to the ground.

"That's it?" Shai-ster grimaced.

Don Bruce frowned at the wand.

"That's funny. When the guy back there did it, he got a rainbow."

He pointed the wand at the ground and shook it . . . and three blades materialized out of thin air, lancing into the dust at our feet.

"Careful!" Shai-ster warned, hopping back out of range. "You'd better read the instructions on that thing."

"I don't need instructions," Don Bruce insisted. "I'm a fairy godfather. I know what I'm doing."

As he spoke, he gestured emphatically with the wand, and a jet of flame narrowly missed one of the bodyguards.

". . . But this can wait," Don Bruce concluded, tucking the wand into his waistband. "We've got business to discuss."

"Yes. We were just . . ." Shai-ster began.

"Shuddup! I'm talking to Skeeve here."

The force behind Don Bruce's sudden admonishment, combined with the Shai-ster's quick obedience, made me hastily revise my opinion of the Mob leader. Strange or not, he was a force to be recognized.

"Now then, Mister Skeeve, what's the police situation around here?"

"There aren't any."

Shaister's eyebrows shot up.

"Then how do they enforce the laws?" he asked, forgetting himself.

"As far as I can tell, there are no laws either."

"How 'bout that, Shai-ster?" Don Bruce laughed. "No police, no laws, no lawyers. You'd be in trouble if you were born here."

I started to ask what a lawyer was, but the godfather saved me from my own ignorance by plunging into the next question.

"How about politicians?"

"None."

"Unions?"

"None."

"Bookies?"

"Lots," I admitted. "This is the gambling capital of the dimensions. As near as I can tell, though, they all operate independently. There's no central organization."

Don Bruce rubbed his hands together gleefully.

"You listening to this, Shai-ster? This is some world Mister Skeeve is givin' us here."

"He's not giving it to us," Shai-ster corrected. "He's offering *access* to it."

"That's right," I said quickly. "Exploiting it is up to your organization. Now, if you don't think your boys can handle it. . . ."

"We can handle it. A layout like this? It's a piece of cake."

Guido and Nunzio exchanged nervous glances, but held their silence as Don Bruce continued.

"Now if I understand this right, what you want in return for letting us into this territory is that we lay off Big Julie and Possiltum. Right?"

I count real good up to three.

"And me," I added. "No 'getting even with the guy who thrashed our army plans,' no 'join the Mob or die' pressure. I'm an independent operator and happy to stay that way."

"Sure, sure," Don Bruce waved. "Now that we've seen how you operate, no reason we can't eat out of the same bowl. If anything, we owe you a favor for opening up a new area to our organization."

Somehow, that worried me.

"Um . . . tell you what. I don't want any credit for this . . . inside the Mob or outside. Right now, nobody but us knows I had a hand in this. Let's keep it that way, okay?"

"If that's what you want," Don Bruce shrugged. "I'll just tell the Big Boys you're too rough for us to tangle with, and that's why we're going to leave you alone. Anytime our paths cross, we go ahead with your approval or we back off. Okay?"

"That's what I want."

"Deal?"

"Deal."

We shook hands ceremoniously.

"Very well," I said. "Here's what you need to travel between here and home."

I fished the D-Hopper out of my sleeve.

"This setting is for home. This one is for here. Push this button to travel."

"What about the other settings?" Shai-ster asked.

"Remember the magic wand?" I countered. "Without instructions, you could get lost with this thing. I mean, *really* lost."

"Come on, boys," Don Bruce said, setting the D-Hopper. "We gotta hurry home. There's a world here to conquer, so we gotta get started before somebody else beats us to it. Mister Skeeve, a pleasure doin' business with you."

A second later, they were gone.

I should have been elated, having finally eliminated one set of problems from my horizon. I wasn't.

Don Bruce's last comment about world conquering reminded me of Queen Hemlock's plans. Now that the Mob was neutralized, I had other problems to solve. As soon as I got back to the palace, I would have to . . .

Then it hit me.

The Mob representatives had taken the D-Hopper with them when they left. That thing was my only route back to Klah! I was stranded at the Bazaar with no way back to my own dimension!

Chapter Twelve:

"I'm making this up as I go along!"
—I. JONES

BUT I didn't panic. Why should I?

Sure, I was in a bit of a mess, but if there was one place in all the dimensions I could be confident of finding help, it was here at the Bazaar. Anything could be had here for a price, and thanks to Aahz's training, I had made a point of stocking my pouch with money prior to our departure from Klah.

Aahz!

It suddenly occurred to me that I hadn't thought about my old mentor for days. The crises that had erupted shortly after his departure had occupied my mind to an extent where there was no time or energy left for brooding. Except for the occasional explanation of his absence, Aahz was playing no part in my life currently. I was successfully handling things without him.

Well . . .

Okay. I had successfully handled *some* things without him . . . the Mob, for example. Of course, the training he had gotten me into earlier in our relationship had also provided me with confidence under fire . . . another much-needed commodity these days.

"Face it, kid," I said to myself in my best imitation of Aahz. "You owe a lot to your old mentor."

Right. A lot. Like not making him ashamed of his prize pupil . . . say by leaving a job half done.

With new resolve, I addressed my situation. First, I had to get back to Klah . . . or should I look for a solution right here?

Rather than lose time to indecision, I compromised. With a few specific questions to the nearest vendor, I set a course for my eventual destination, keeping an eye out as I went for something that would help me solve the Queen Hemlock problem.

This trip through the Bazaar was different from my earlier visits. Before, my experience had been of wishing for more time to study the displays at leisure while hurrying to keep up with Aahz. This time, it was me that was pushing the pace, dismissing display after display with a casual "interesting, but no help with today's problem." Things seemed to have a different priority when responsibility for the crisis was riding on *my* shoulders.

Of course, I didn't know what I was looking for. I just knew that trick wands and instant thunderstorms weren't it. Out of desperation, I resorted to logic.

To recognize the solution, I needed to know the problem. The problem was that Queen Hemlock was about to marry me instead of Rodrick. Scratch that. Massha was bringing Rodrick back, and I couldn't help her. I just had to believe she could do it. The problem was Queen Hemlock.

Whether she married me or Rodrick, she was determined to use Possiltum's military strength to wage a war of expansion. If her husband, whoever it was, tried to oppose her, he would find himself conveniently dead.

Killing the Queen would be one solution, but somehow I shrank from cold-blooded murder . . . or hot-blooded murder for that matter. No. What was needed was something to throw a scare into her. A big scare.

The answer walked past me before I recognized it. Fortunately, it was moving slowly, so I turned and caught up with it in just a few steps.

Answers come in many shapes and sizes. This one was in the form of a Deveel with a small tray display hung by a strap around his neck.

"What you just said, was it true?"

The Deveel studied me.

"I said, 'Rings. One size fits all. Once on, never off.' "

"That's right. Is it true?"

"Of course. Each of my rings are pre-spelled. Once you put it on, it self-adjusts so that it won't come off, even if you want it to."

"Great. I'll take two."

". . . Because to lose a ring of such value would be tragedy indeed. Each one worth a king's ransom. . . ."

I rolled my eyes.

"Look," I interrupted. "I know it's a tradition of the Bazaar to bargain, but I'm in a hurry. How much for two? Bottom price."

He thought for a moment and named a figure. My training came to the fore and I made a counteroffer one-tenth of his.

"Hey! You said 'no haggling,' " he protested. "Who do you think you are?"

Well, it was worth a try. According to Massha, I was getting a bit of a reputation at the Bazaar.

"I think I'm the Great Skeeve, since you asked."

". . . And the camel you rode in on," the vendor sneered. "Everyone knows the Great Skeeve isn't a Pervert."

The disguise! I had forgotten about it completely. With a mental wave, I restored my normal appearance.

"No, I'm a Klahd," I smiled. "And for your information, that's Pervect!"

"You mean you're really . . . no, you must be. No one else would voluntarily look like a Klahd . . . or defend Perverts . . . excuse me, Pervects."

"Now that that's established," I yawned, "how much for two of your rings?"

"Here," he said, thrusting the tray forward. "Take your pick, with my compliments. I won a bundle betting on your team at the Great Game. All I ask is permission to say that you use my wares."

It was with a great deal of satisfaction that I made my selection and continued on my way. It was nice to have a reputation, but nicer to earn it. Those two little baubles now riding in my pouch were going to get me out of the Possiltum dilemma . . . if I got back in time . . . and if Massha had found the King.

Those sobering thoughts brought my hat size back to normal in a hurry. The time to gloat was after the battle, not before. Plans aren't victories, as I should be the first to know.

With panic once again nipping at my heels, I quickened my pace until I was nearly running by the time I reached my final destination: the Yellow Crescent Inn.

Bursting through the door of the Bazaar's leading fast food establishment, I saw that it was empty of customers except for a troll munching on a table in the corner.

Terrific.

I was expecting to deal with Gus, the gargoyle proprietor, but I'd settle for the troll.

"Skeeve!" the troll exclaimed. "I say, this is a surprise. What brings you to the Bazaar?"

"Later, Chumly. Right now I need a lift back to Klah. Are you busy with anything?"

The troll set his half-eaten table to one side and raised the eyebrow over one mismatched moon eye.

"Not to be picky about formality," he said, "but what happened to 'Hello, Chumly. How are you?' "

"I'm sorry. I'm in a bit of a hurry. Can we just. . . ."

"Skeeve! How's it going, handsome?"

A particularly curvaceous bundle of green-haired loveliness had just emerged from the ladies' room.

"Oh. Hi, Tananda. How 'bout it, Chumly?"

Tananda's smile of welcome disappeared, to be replaced by a puzzled frown.

" 'Oh. Hi, Tananda?' " she repeated, shooting a look at the troll. "Does anything strike you as strange about that rather low-key greeting, big brother?"

"No stranger than the greeting I just got," Chumly confided. "Just off-hand, I'd say that either our young friend here has forgotten his manners completely, or he's gotten himself into a spot of trouble."

Their eyes locked and they nodded.

"Trouble," they said together.

"Cute," I grimaced. "Okay, so I'm in a mess. I'm not asking you to get involved. In fact, I think I've got it worked out myself. All I want is for you to pop me back to Klah."

Brother and sister stepped to my side.

"Certainly," Chumly smiled. "You don't mind if we tag along, though, do you?"

"But I didn't ask you to . . ."

"When have you had to ask for our help before, handsome?" Tananda scolded, slipping an arm around my waist. "We're your friends, remember?"

"But I think I've got it handled . . ."

". . . In which case, having us along won't hurt," the troll insisted.

"Unless, of course, something goes wrong," Tananda supplied. "In which case, we might be able to lend a hand."

". . . And if the three of us can't handle it, we'll be there to pull you out again," Chumly finished.

I should have known better than to try to argue with the two of them when they were united.

"But . . . if . . . well, thanks," I managed. "I didn't really expect this. I mean, you don't even know what the trouble is."

"You can tell us later," Tananda said firmly, starting her conjuring to move us through the dimensions. "Incidentally, where's Aahz?"

"That's part of the problem," I sighed.

And we were back!

Not just back on Klah, back in my own quarters in the palace. As luck would have it, we weren't alone. Someday I'll have time to figure out if it was good luck or bad.

The King was trussed up hand and foot on my bed, while Massha and J. R. Grimble were each enjoying a goblet of wine, and apparently each other's company. At least, that was the scene when we arrived. Once Massha and Tananda set eyes on each other, the mood changed dramatically.

"Slut," my new apprentice hissed.

"No-talent mechanic," Tananda shot back.

"Is that freak on our payroll?" Grimble interrupted, staring at Chumly.

"Spoken like a true bean-counter," the troll sneered.

I tried to break it up.

"If we can just . . ."

That brought Grimble's attention to me.

"You!" he gasped. "But if you're Skeeve, then who's. . . ."

"King Rodrick of Possiltum," I supplied, nodding to the bound figure on the bed. "And now that everybody knows each other, can you all shut up while I tell you what our next move is?"

Chapter Thirteen:

"Marriage, being a lifelong venture, must be approached with care and caution."

—BLUEBEARD

THE wedding went off without a hitch.

I don't known why I had been worried. There were no interruptions, no missed lines, nobody protested or even coughed at the wrong time. As was previously noted, Queen Hemlock had handled the planning to the last minute detail . . . except for a few surprises we were holding back.

That's why I was worried! My cronies and I knew that as gaudy and overdone as the Royal Wedding was, it was only the warm-up act for the main event. There was also the extra heat on me of knowing that I hadn't shared *all* of my plans with my co-conspirators. It seemed that was another bad habit I had picked up from Aahz.

Grimble and Badaxe were at their usual places as mismatched bookends to the throne, while Chumly, Tananda, Massha, and I, courtesy of my disguise spells and Badaxe's pull as general, were lined up along the foot of the throne as bodyguards. Everything was set to go . . . if we ever got the time!

As dignitary after dignitary stepped forward to offer his or her congratulations and gifts, I found little to occupy my thoughts except how many things could go wrong with my little scheme. I had stuck my neck out a long way with my plan, and if it didn't work, a lot of people would be affected, starting with the king and subjects of Possiltum.

The more I thought, the more I worried until, instead of wishing the dignitaries would hurry, I actually found myself hoping they would take forever and preserve this brief moment of peace.

Of course, no sooner did I start hoping things would last then they were over. The last well-wisher was filing out and the Queen herself rising to leave when Grimble and Badaxe left their customary positions and stepped before the throne.

"Before you go, my dear," Rodrick said, "our retainers wish to extend their compliments."

Queen Hemlock frowned slightly, but resumed her seat.

"The Chancellor of the Exchequer stands ready to support their majesties in any way," Grimble began. "Of course, even with the new influx of wealth into the treasury, we must watch needless expenses. As always, I stand ready to set the example in cost savings, and so have decided that to purchase a present for you equal to my esteem would be a flagrant and unnecessary expense, and therefore . . ."

"Yes, yes, Grimble," the King interrupted. "We understand and appreciate your self-sacrifice. General Badaxe?"

Grimble hesitated, then yielded the floor to his rival.

"I am a fighting man, not a speechmaker," the General said abruptly. "The army stands ready to support the kingdom and the throne of Possiltum. As for myself . . . here is my present.''

He removed the axe from his belt and laid it on the stairs before the throne.

Whether he was offering his pet weapon or his personal allegiance, I found the gesture eloquent beyond words.

''Thank you, General Badaxe, Grimble,'' Queen Hemlock said loftily. ''I'm sure I can . . .''

''My dear,'' the King interrupted softly. ''There *is* another retainer.''

And I was on.

Screwing up my courage, I dropped my disguise and stepped before the throne.

''Your majesties, the Great Skeeve gives you his congratulations on this happy event.''

The Queen was no fool. For one beat her eyes popped open and on the next she was staring at the King. You could almost hear her thoughts: ''If the Magician is there, then the man I just married is . . .''

''That's right, your majesty. As you yourself said in our earlier conversations, 'Royalty has married royalty.' ''

While it might have been nice dramatically to savor that moment, I noticed the Queen's eyes were narrowing thoughtfully, so I hurried on.

''Before you decide how to express your joy,'' I warned, ''perhaps I should explain *my* gift to the throne.''

Now the thoughtful gaze was on me. I expressed my own joy by sweating profusely.

''My gift is the wedding rings now worn by both king and queen. I hope you like them, because they won't come off.''

Queen Hemlock made one brief attempt to remove her ring, then her eyes were on me again. This time, the gaze wasn't thoughtful.

"Just as the fate of the kingdom of Possiltum is linked to the throne, as of the moment you donned those rings, your fates are linked to each other. By the power of a spell so simple it cannot be broken or countered, when one of you dies, so does the other."

The Queen didn't like that at all, and even the King showed a small frown wrinkle on his forehead, as if contemplating something he had not previously considered. That was my signal to clarify things for him . . . that there *was* an implication to the rings that I hadn't mentioned to him.

"This is not intended as a 'one-sided' gift, for just as Queen Hemlock must now protect the health and well-being of her king, so must King Rodrick defend his queen against all dangers . . . *all* dangers."

The King was on his feet now, eyes flashing.

"What is that supposed to mean, Lord Magician?"

As adept as I was at becoming at courtly speech, there were things which I felt were best said in the vernacular.

"It means if you or anybody else kills her, say, on your orders, then, *you're* dead. Now *SIT DOWN AND LISTEN!!*"

All the anger and frustration I had felt since figuring out the King was trying to double-cross me, but had been too busy to express, found its vent in that outburst. It worked. The King sank back into his chair, pale and slightly shaken.

I wasn't done, though. I had been through a lot, and a few words weren't enough to settle my mind.

"Since I accepted this assignment, I've heard nothing but how ruthless and ambitious Queen Hemlock is. Well, that may be true, *BUT SHE ISN'T GETTING*

ANY PRIZE EITHER! Right now, *King* Rodrick, I have more respect for her than I have for you. *She* didn't abandon her kingdom in the middle of a crisis.''

I began to pace back and forth before the thrones as I warmed to my topic.

"Everybody talks about 'our duty to the throne.' It's the guiding directive in the walk-a-day life of commoners. What never gets mentioned is 'the throne's duty to the people.' ''

I paused and pointed directly at the King.

"I sat in that chair for a while. It's a lot of fun, deciding people's lives for them. Power is heady, and the fringe benefits are great! All that bowing and scraping, not to mention one heck of a wardrobe. Still, it's a job like any other, and with any job you sometimes have to do things you don't like. Badaxe doesn't just parade and review his troops, he has to train them and lead them into battle . . . you know, as in 'I could get killed out here' battle. Grimble spends ungodly hours poring over those numbers of his for the privilege of standing at your side.

"Any job has its pluses and minuses, and if the minuses outweight the pluses, you screw up your courage and quit . . . unless, of course, you're King Rodrick. Then, instead of abdicating and turning the pluses and minuses over to someone else, you stick someone else with doing the job in your name and sneak out a back door. Maybe that's how people do their jobs where you were raised, but I think it's conduct a peasant would be ashamed of.''

I faced them, hands defiantly on my hips.

"Well, I've done *my* job. The kingdom has been protected from the immediate threat. With any luck, you two will learn to work together. I trust King Rodrick can dilute the queen's ambition. I only hope that Queen

Hemlock's fiery spirit can put a little more spine and courage into the King."

This time it was Queen Hemlock who was on her feet.

"Are you going to let him talk to you like that, Roddie? You're the king. Nobody pushes a king around."

"Guards!" Rodrick said tightly. "Seize that man."

It had worked! King and Queen were united against a common foe . . . me! Now all I had to do was survive it.

One more mind pass, and my comrades stood exposed as the outworlders they were.

Queen Hemlock, unaccustomed to my dealings with demons, dropped into her seat with a small gasp. The King simply scowled as he realized the real reason for the presence of my friends.

"Your Majesties," Badaxe said, stepping forward. "I am sworn to protect the throne and would willingly lay down my life in your defense. I do not see a physical threat here, however. If anything, it occurs to me both throne and kingdom would be strengthened if the Great Skeeve's words were heard and heeded."

"I am not a fighting man," Grimble said, joining Badaxe, "so my duty here is passive. I must add, though, that I also feel the Lord Magician's words have merit and should be said to every ruler."

His eyes narrowed and he turned to face me.

"I challenge, though, whether they should be said by a retainer to the court. One of our first duties is to show respect to the throne, in word and manner."

"That much we agree on, Grimble," Badaxe nodded, adding his glare to the many focused on me.

"Strange as it may sound," I said, "I agree, too. For that reason, I am hereby tendering my resignation as Court Magician of Possiltum. The kingdom is now secure militarily and financially, and in my opinion there is no point in it bearing the expense of a full-time magician . . . especially one who has been insolent to the throne. There is no need to discuss severance pay. The King's reward for my last assignment, coupled with the monies I have already received from the Exchequer, will serve my needs adequately. I will simply gather my things and depart.''

I saw Grimble blanch slightly when he realized that I would not be returning his bribe. I had faith in his ability to hide anything in his stacks of numbered sheets, though.

With only the slightest of nods to the throne, I gathered my entourage with my eyes and left.

Everything had gone perfectly. I couldn't have asked for the proceedings to have turned out better. As such, I was puzzled as to why I was sweat-drenched and shaking like a leaf by the time I reached my own quarters.

Chapter Fourteen:

"Some farewells are easier than others."
—P. MARLOWE

"So, where do you go from here?" Tananda asked.

She and Chumly were helping me pack. We had all agreed that having incurred the combined wrath of the King and Queen, it would be wisest to delay my departure as little as possible. Massha was off seeing to Gleep and Buttercup as well as saying her goodbyes to Badaxe.

"I don't really know," I admitted. "I was serious when I said I had accumulated enough wealth for a while. I'll probably hole up someplace and practice my magic for a while . . . maybe at that inn Aahz and I used to use as a home base."

"I say, why don't you tag along with little sister and me?" Chumly suggested. "We usually operate out of the Bazaar at Deva. It wouldn't be a bad place for you to keep your hand in, magik-wise."

It flashed through my mind that the Mob must have started its infiltration of the Bazaar by now. It also occurred to me that, in the pre-wedding rush, I hadn't told Tananda or Chumly about that particular portion of the caper. Having remembered, I found myself reluctant to admit my responsibility for what they'd find on their return.

"I dunno, Chumly," I hedged. "You two travel pretty light. I've got so much stuff, I'd probably be better off settling down somewhere permanent."

It was a pretty weak argument, but the troll seemed to accept it . . . maybe because he could see that mountain of gear we were accumulating, trying to clear my quarters.

"Well, think it over. We'd be glad to have you. You're not a bad sort to have around in a tight spot."

"I'll say," Tananda agreed with a laugh. "Where did you find those rings, anyway?"

"Bought them from a street vendor at the Bazaar."

"On Deva?" Chumly said with a frown. "Two spelled rings like that must have set you back a pretty penny. Are you *sure* you have enough money left?"

Now it was my turn to laugh.

"First of all, they aren't spelled. That was just a bluff I was running on their royal majesties. The rings are plain junk jewelry . . . and I got them for free."

"Free?"

Now Tananda was frowning.

"Nobody gets anything for free at the Bazaar."

"No, really. They were free . . . well, the vendor did get my permission to say that I use his wares, but that's the same as free, isn't it? I mean, I didn't pay him any money."

As I spoke, I found myself suddenly uncertain of my "good deal." One of my earliest lessons about dealing with Deveels was "If you think you've made a good deal with a Deveel, first count your fingers, then your limbs, then your relatives. . . ."

"Permission to use your name?" Tananda echoed. "For two lousy rings? No percentage or anything? Didn't Aahz ever teach you about endorsements?"

There was a soft *BAMPH* in the air.

"Is someone taking my name in vain?"

And Aahz was there, every green scaly inch of him, making his entrance as casually as if he had just stepped out.

Of the three of us, I was the first to recover from my surprise. Well, at least I found my voice.

"Aahz!"

"Hi, kid. Miss me?"

"But, Aahz!"

I didn't know if I should laugh or cry. What I really wanted to do was embrace him and never let go. Of course, now that he was back, I would do no such thing. I mean, our relationship had never been big in the emotional displays department.

"What's the matter with everybody?" my mentor demanded. "You all act like you never expected to see me again."

"We . . . Aahz! I . . ."

"We didn't," Tananda said flatly, saving me from making an even bigger fool of myself.

"What little sister means," Chumly put in, "is that it was our belief that your nephew, Rupert, had no intention of letting you return from Perv."

Aahz gave a derisive snort.

"Rupert? That upstart? Don't tell me anybody takes him seriously."

"Well, maybe not if your powers were in full force," Tananda said, "but as things are . . ."

"Rupert?" Aahz repeated. "You two have known me a long time, right? Then you should get it through your heads that nobody holds me against my will."

Somehow that quote sounded familiar. Still, I was so glad to have Aahz back, I would have agreed to anything just then.

"Yeah!" I chimed in eagerly. "This is Aahz! *Nobody* pushes him around."

"There!" my mentor grinned. "As much as I hate to

agree with a mere apprentice, the kid knows what he's talking about . . . this time.''

Chumly and Tananda looked at each other with that special gaze that brother and sister use to communicate non-verbally.

"You know, big brother,'' Tananda said, "this mutual admiration society is getting a bit much for my stomach. How about you?''

"Ectually,'' the troll responded. "I wasn't hearing all that much *mutual* admiration. Somehow the phrase 'mere apprentice' sticks in my mind.''

"Oh, come on, you two,'' Aahz waved. "Get real, huh? I mean, we all like the kid, but we also know he's a trouble magnet. I've never met anyone who needs looking after as badly as he does. Speaking of which . . .''

He turned his yellow eyes on me with that speculative look of his.

". . . I notice you're both here . . . *and* I definitely heard my name as I phased in. What I need more than fond 'hellos' is a quick update as to exactly what kind of a mess we have to bail the Great Skeeve out of this time.''

I braced myself for a quick but loud lesson about "endorsements,'' whatever that was, but the troll surprised me.

"No mess,'' he said, leaning back casually. "Little sister and I just dropped by for a visit. In fact, we were just getting ready to leave.''

"Really?'' my mentor sounded both surprised and suspicious. "Just a visit? No trouble?''

"Well, there was a *little* trouble,'' Tananda admitted. "Something to do with the King. . . .''

"I knew it!'' Aahz chortled, rubbing his hands together.

". . . But Skeeve here handled it himself,'' she finished pointedly. "Currently, there are no problems at all."

"Oh."

Strangely, Aahz seemed a bit disappointed.

"Well, I guess I owe you two some thanks, then. I really appreciate your watching over Skeeve here while I was gone. He can . . ."

"I don't think you're listening, Aahz," Chumly said, looking at the ceiling. "Skeeve handled the trouble. We just watched."

"Oh, we would have pitched in if things got tight," Tananda supplied. "You know, the way we do for *you*, Aahz. As it turned out, we weren't needed. Your 'mere apprentice' was more than equal to the task."

"Finished the job rather neatly, you know?" the troll added. "In fact, I'm hard pressed to recall when I've seen a nasty situation dealt with as smoothly or with as little fuss."

"All right, all right," Aahz grimaced. "I get the message. You can fill me in on the details later. Right now, the kid and I have some big things to discuss . . . and I mean *big*."

"Like what?" I frowned.

"Well, I've been giving it a lot of thought, and I figure it's about time we left Possiltum and moved on."

"Um, Aahz?" I said.

"I know, I know," he waved. "You think you need practice. You do, but you've come a long way. This whole thing with the trouble you handled only proves my point. You're ready to . . ."

"Aahz?"

"All right. I know you've got friends and duties here, but eventually you have to leave the nest. You'll just have to trust my judgment and experience to know when the time is right to . . ."

"I've already quit!"

Aahz stopped in midsentence and stared at me.

"You have?" he blinked.

I nodded and pointed at the pile of gear we had been packing. He studied it for a moment as if he didn't believe what he was seeing.

"Oh," he said at last. "Oh well, in that case, I'll just duck over to talk to Grimble and discuss your severance pay. He's a tight-fisted bird, but if I can't shake five hundred out of him, I'll know the reason why."

"I know the reason why," I said carefully.

Aahz rolled his eyes.

"Look, kid. This is *my* field of expertise, remember? If you go into a bargaining session aiming low, they'll walk all over you. You've got to . . ."

"I've already negotiated for a thousand!"

This time, Aahz's "freeze" was longer . . . and he didn't look at me.

"A thousand?" he said finally. "In gold?"

"Plus a hefty bonus from the King himself," Tananda supplied helpfully.

"We've been trying to tell you, Aahz old boy," Chumly smiled. "Skeeve here has been doing just fine without you."

"I see."

Aahz turned away and stared silently out the window.

I'll admit to being a bit disappointed. I mean, maybe I hadn't done a first-rate job, but a *little* bit of congratulations would have been nice. The way my mentor was acting, you'd think he. . . .

Then it hit me. Like a runaway war-chariot it hit me. Aahz was jealous! More than that, he was hurt!

I could see it now with crystal clarity. Up until now I had been blinded by Aahz's arrogant self-confidence, but suddenly the veil was parted.

Aahz's escape from Perv wasn't nearly as easy as he

was letting on. There had been a brawl—physical, verbal, or magikal—some hard feelings, and some heavy promises made or broken. He had forced his way back to Klah with one thing on his mind: his apprentice . . . his *favorite* apprentice, was in trouble. Upon returning, what was his reception? Not only was I not in trouble, for all appearances, I was doing better without him!

Tananda and Chumly were still at it, merrily chattering back and forth about how great I was. While I appreciated their support, I wished desperately I could think of a way of getting it through to them that what they were really doing was twisting a knife in Aahz.

"Umm . . . Aahz?" I interrupted. "When you've got a minute, there *are* a few things I need your advice on."

"Like what?" came the muffled response. "From the sound of things, you don't need anybody, much less a teacher with no powers of his own."

Tananda caught it immediately. Her gadfly manner dropped away like a mask and she signaled desperately to Chumly. The troll was not insensitive, though. His reaction was to catch my eye with a pleading gaze.

It was up to me. Terrific.

"Well, like . . . um."

And Massha exploded into the room.

"Everything's ready downstairs, hot stuff, and . . . oh! Hi there, green and scaly. Thought you were gone for good."

Aahz spun around, his eyes wide.

"Massha?" he stammered. "What are you doing here?"

"Didn't the man of the hour here tell you?" she smiled, batting her expansive eyelashes. "I'm his new apprentice."

"Apprentice?" Aahz echoed, his old fire creeping into his voice.

"Um . . . that's one of the things I wanted to talk to

you about, Aahz," I smiled meekly.

"Apprentice?" he repeated, as if he hadn't heard. "Kid, you and I have got to talk . . . NOW!"

"Okay, Aahz. As soon as I. . . ."

"Now!"

Yep. Aahz was back.

"Um, if you'll excuse us, folks, Aahz and I have to . . ."

For the second time, there was a *BAMPH* in the room.

This one was louder, which was understandable, as there were more beings involved. Specifically, there were now four Deveels standing in the room . . . and they didn't look happy.

"We seek the Great Skeeve," one of them boomed.

My heart sank. Could my involvement with the Mob have been discovered so fast?

"Who's asking?"

Aahz casually placed his bulk between me and the intruders. Tananda and Chumly were also on their feet, and Massha was edging sideways to get a clear field of fire. Terrific. All I needed to complete my day was to have my friends soap up the trouble I had started.

"We are here representing the merchants of the Bazaar on the Deva, seeking an audience with the Great Skeeve."

"About what?" my mentor challenged.

The Deveel fixed him with an icy glare.

"We seek the Great Skeeve, not idle chit-chat with a Pervert."

"Well, this particular Per-*vect* happens to be the Great Skeeve's business manager, and he doesn't waste his time with Deveels unless *I* clear them."

I almost said something, but changed my mind. Concerned or not, this was not the time to take a conversation away from Aahz.

The Deveel hesitated, then shrugged.

"There is a new difficulty at the Bazaar," he said. "A group of organized criminals has gained access to our dimension threatening to disrupt the normal flow of business unless they are paid a percentage of our profits."

Tananda and Chumly exchanged glances, while Massha raised an eyebrow at me. I studied the ceiling with extreme care. Aahz alone was unruffled.

"Tough. So what does that have to do with the Great Skeeve?" he demanded.

Anticipating the answer, I tried to decide whether I should fight or run.

"Isn't it obvious?" the Deveel frowned. "We wish to retain his services to combat this threat. From what we can tell, he's the only magician around up to the job."

That one stopped me. Of all the strange turns events could have taken, this had to be the most unanticipated and . . . well, bizarre!

"I see," Aahz murmured, a nasty gleam in his eye. "You realize, of course, that the Great Skeeve's time is valuable and that such a massive undertaking would require equally massive remuneration?"

Every alarm in my system went off.

"Um . . . Aahz?"

"Shut up, k . . . I mean, be patient, Master Skeeve. This matter should be settled in a moment."

I couldn't watch.

Instead, *I* went to the window and stared out. Listening over my shoulder, I heard Aahz name an astronomical figure, and realized there might be a way out of this yet. If Aahz was greedy enough, and the Deveels stingy enough . . .

"Done!" said the spokesman.

". . . Of course, that's only an advance," Aahz

pressed. ''A full rendering will have to wait until the job is completed.''

''Done,'' came the reply.

''. . . And that is the fee only. Expenses will be reimbursed separately.''

''Done! The advance will be awaiting your arrival. Anything else?''

In tribute to the Deveel's generosity, Aahz was unable to think of any other considerations to gouge out of them.

There was another *BAMPH*, and the delegation was gone.

''How about that!'' Aahz crowed. ''I finally put one over on the Deveels!''

''What's that thing you always say about anyone who thinks they've gotten a good deal from a Deveel, Aahz?'' Tananda asked sweetly.

''Later,'' my mentor ordered. ''Right now we've got to get our things together and pop over to the Bazaar to scout the opposition.''

''We already know what the opposition is.''

''How's that, kid?''

I turned to face him.

''The opposition is the Mob. You remember, the organized crime group that was sponsoring Big Julie's army?''

A frown crossed Aahz's face as he regarded me closely.

''And how did you come by that little tidbit of information, if I may ask?''

I regarded him right back.

''That's the other little thing I wanted your advice on.''

Chapter Fifteen:

"In a war against organized crime, survival is a hit or myth proposition."

—M. BOLAN

"Now let me see if I've got this right," Aahz scowled, pacing back and forth in front of our worried gazes. "What we've got to do is keep the Mob from taking over the Bazaar, without letting them know we're opposing them or the Deveels know we were the ones who loosed the Mob on the Bazaar in the first place. Right?"

"You can do it, Aahz," I urged eagerly.

This time, it required no false enthusiasm on my part. While I had done an adequate job operating on my own, when it came to premeditated deviousness, I was quick to acknowledge my master. There might be someone out there in the multitude of dimensions better than Aahz at finding under-handed ways out of dilemmas, but I haven't met them yet.

"Of course I can do it," my mentor responded with a confident wink. "I just want everyone to admit it isn't going to be easy. All this talk about the Great Skeeve has made me a little insecure."

"A little?" Tananda smirked.

"I think it's a bit of all right," Chumly said, nudging

113

his sister with an elbow. "I've always heard how formidable Aahz is when he swings into action. I, for one, am dying to see him handle this rather sticky situation all by himself."

Aahz's shoulders sagged slightly as he heaved a small sigh.

"Whoa! Stop! Perhaps in my enthusiasm I overspoke. What I *meant* to say is that my slimy but agile mind can provide a *plan* to pull off this assignment. Of course, the execution of said plan will rely upon abilities and goodwill of my worthy colleagues. Is that better, Chumly?"

"Quite," the troll nodded.

"Now that that's settled," Gus interrupted impatiently, "can we get on with it? This *is* my place of business, you know, and the longer I keep the place closed, the more money I lose."

For those of you who missed the earlier references, Gus is a gargoyle. He is also the owner/proprietor of the Yellow Crescent Inn, the Bazaar's leading fast-food establishment and our current field headquarters. Like Chumly and Tananda, he's helped me out of a couple scrapes in the past and, as soon as he heard about our current crisis, volunteered again. Like anyone who earns their living at the Bazaar, however, he habitually keeps one eye on the cash register. Even though he had closed his doors to give us a base of operations for the upcoming campaign, there was still a reflexive bristling over missed profits.

An idea struck me.

"Relax, Gus," I ordered. "Come up with a daily figure for your normal trade, bump it for a decent profit, and we'll reimburse you when this thing's over."

"What!" my mentor screeched, losing momentary control. "Are you out of your mind, kid? Who do you think is paying for this, anyway?''

"The merchants of Deva," I answered calmly.
"We're on an expense account, remember? I think rent-
ing a place while we're on assignment isn't an unreason-
able expense, do you?''

"Oh. Right. Sorry, Gus. Old reflexes."

Aahz's confusion was momentary. Then his eyes narrowed thoughtfully.

"In fact, if we put all of you on retainer, your help
will fall under the heading of 'consultant fees' and never
come near our own profits. I like it.''

"Before you get too carried away," Tananda put in
quickly, "I think big brother and I would rather work
for a piece of the action than on a flat fee.''

"But, honey," Massha blinked, "You haven't even
heard his plan yet. What makes you think a percentage
will net you more than a fee? . . . just between us girls?''

"Just between us girls," Tananda winked, "you've
never worked with Aahz before. I have, and while he
may not be the pleasantest being to team with, I have
unshakeable faith in his profit margins.''

"Now that we're on the subject," Aahz said, staring
hard at Massha, "we never *have* worked together
before, so let's get the rules straight early on. I've got
my own style, see, and it usually doesn't allow much
time for 'please' and 'thank you' and explanations. As
long as you do what you're told, when you're told, we'll
get along fine. Right?''

"Wrong!"

My reply popped out before Massha could form her
own response. I was vaguely aware that the room had
gotten very quiet, but most of my attention was on Aahz
as he slowly cranked his head around to lock gazes with
me.

"Now look, kid. . . ." he began dangerously.

"No, *you* look, Aahz," I exploded. "I may be your apprentice, but Massha is *mine*. Now if she wants to dump that agreement and sign on with you, fine and dandy. But until she does, she's *my* student and *my* responsibility. If you think she can help, then you suggest it to me and *I* decide whether she's up to it. There's one lesson you've drummed into my head over and over, mentor mine, whether you meant to or not. Nobody leans on your apprentice but you . . . nobody! If you didn't want to teach that lesson, then maybe you'd better be more careful with the example you set the next time you take on an apprentice."

"I see," Aahz murmured softly. "Getting pretty big for your britches, aren't you, kid?"

"Not really. I'm very much aware of how little I know, thank you. But this is my assignment, or at least it was accepted in my name, and I mean to give it my best shot . . . however inadequate that might be. Now for that assignment, I need your help, Aahz . . . heck, I'll always probably need your help. You're my teacher and I've got a lot to learn. But, I'm not going to roll over and die without it. If getting your help means turning my assignment and my apprentice over to you, then forget it. I'll just have to try to handle things without you."

"You'll get your brains beat out."

"Maybe. I didn't say I'd win, just that I'd try my best. *You* bring out my best, Aahz. You push me into things that scare me, but so far I've muddled through somehow. I *need* your help, but I don't *have* to have it. Even if you don't want to admit it to me, I think you should admit it to yourself."

With that, we both lapsed into silence.

Me, I couldn't think of anything else to say. Up until now, I had been carried along by my anger and Aahz's responses. All of a sudden, my mentor wasn't responding. Instead, he stared at me with expressionless yellow eyes, not saying a thing.

It was more than a little unnerving. If there is one characteristic of Aahz's I could always count on, it was that he was expressive. Whether with facial expression, gestures, grunts, or verbal explosions, my mentor usually let everyone in the near vicinity know what he felt or thought about any event or opinion expressed. Right now, though, I didn't know if he was about to explode or just walk away.

I began having regrets over instigating this confrontation. Then I toughened up. What I had said was right and needed to be said. It flashed across my mind that I could lose Aahz over this argument. My resolve wavered. Right or not, I could have said it better . . . gentler. At least I could have picked a time when all our friends weren't watching and listening. Maybe. . . .

Aahz turned away abruptly, shifting his stance to face Tananda and Chumly.

"*Now* I'm ready to believe you two," he announced. "The kid here really *did* handle that mess on Klah all by himself, didn't he?"

"That's what we've been trying to tell you, old boy," the troll winked. "Your apprentice is growing up, and seems to us more than capable of standing on his own two feet lately."

"Yeah, I noticed."

He looked at me again, and this time his eyes were expressive. I didn't recognize the expression, but at least there was one.

"Kid . . . Skeeve," he said. "If I've ever wondered why I bothered taking you under my wing, you just gave me the answer. Thanks."

"Um . . . Thanks. I mean, you're welcome. No. I mean . . ."

As always, I was very glib in the face of the unexpected. I had gotten used to weathering Aahz's tirades, but *this* I didn't know how to handle. Fortunately my pet came to my rescue.

"Gleep?" he queried, shaking his head in through the door.

". . . But if you take anything I've showed you, I mean spell one, and teach it to that dragon," my mentor roared, "you and I are going to go a couple rounds. Do we understand each other, apprentice?"

"Yes, Aahz."

Actually, I didn't. Still, this didn't seem like the time to call for a clarification.

"Butt out, Gleep," I ordered. "Go play with Buttercup or something."

"Gleep!" and my dragon's head was gone as fast as it had appeared.

"Say, hot stuff," Massha drawled. "As much as I appreciate your standing up for me, I'm kinda curious to hear what Big Green has for a plan."

"Right!" I nodded, glad to be off the hot seat. "Sorry, Aahz, I didn't mean to interrupt. What's the plan?"

"Well, first," Aahz said, taking his accustomed place as center of attention once more, "I've got a question for Gus. What's the Mob been doing so far to move in?"

"Judging from what I heard," the gargoyle responded, "a bunch of them move in on a merchant and offer to sell him some 'insurance.' You know, 'pay us so much of your revenue and nothing happens to your business.' If anyone's slow to sign up, they arrange a small demonstration of what could go wrong: some 'accidental' breaking of stock or a couple plug-uglies standing outside hassling customers. So far it's been effective. Deveels don't like to lose business."

"Good," my mentor grinned, showing every last one of his numerous pointed teeth. "Then we can beat them."

"How?"

If nothing else, I've gotten quite good at feeding Aahz straight lines.

"Easy. Just ask yourselves this: If you were a Deveel and paid the Mob to protect your business, and things started going wrong anyway, what would you do?"

"I can answer that one," Massha said. "I'd either demand better protection, scream for my money back, or both."

"I don't get it," I frowned. "What's going to happen to a Mob-protected business?"

"We are," Aahz grinned.

"What our strategist is trying to say," Chumly supplied, "is that the best defense is a good offense. Not terribly original, but effective nonetheless."

"You're darn right it's effective," my mentor exclaimed. "Instead of us defending against the Mob, we're going to start a crime wave right here at the Bazaar. Then let's see how good the Mob is at defending against us!"

Chapter Sixteen:

*"It's always easier to destroy than to
create."*
        —ANY GENERAL, ANY ARMY, ANY AGE.

"HEY, Guido! How's it going?"

The big bodyguard spun around, scanning the crowd
to see who had hailed him by name. When he saw me,
his face brightened.

"Mister Skeeve!"

"Never expected to run into you here!" I lied.

From Gus's description, I had known that both
Guido and his cousin Nunzio were part of the Mob's
contingent at the Bazaar. This "chance meeting" was
the result of nearly half a day's worth of searching and
following rumors.

"What are you doing here?" he asked confidentially.
"Shopping for a few little items to wow 'em with back
at Possiltum?"

"Just taking a bit of a vacation. That new queen and
I don't get along so well. I thought things might ease up
if I disappeared for a while."

"Too bad. If you was shoppin', I could line you up
with some 'special deals,' if you know what I mean."

"You guys are really moving in, then?" I marveled.

"How is it going? Any problems?"

"Naw," the bodyguard bragged, puffing out his chest. "You was right. These Deveels are like shopkeepers anywhere. Lean on 'em a little and they fall in line."

"Don't tell me you're handling this all by yourself! I mean I know you're good, but . . ."

"Are you kiddin'? I'm an executive now . . . well, at least a team leader. Both Nunzio and me have a dozen men to order around, courtesy of our 'extensive knowledge of the Bazaar.' Pretty good, huh?"

"You mean you're running the whole operation?"

"That's Shai-ster's job. Me and Nunzio report to him, but it's us gives the orders to the boys."

I looked around expectantly.

"Is your team around? I'd like to meet them."

"Naw. We worked this area a couple days ago. I'm on my way to meet 'em and give out today's assignments. We're going after the area by the livestock pens today."

"How about Nunzio's team?"

"They're about three hours west of here. You know, this is a really big place!"

I put on my most disappointed face.

"Too bad, I would have liked to have met some of the ones who do the *real* work."

"Tell ya' what," Guido exclaimed, "why don't you drop by Fat's Spaghetti Parlor sometimes? That's where we're all hanging out. If we're not there, they can tell you where we are."

"I'll do that. Well, don't work too hard . . . and be careful. These guys can be meaner than they look."

"Piece of cake," he laughed as he headed off.

I was still waving merrily at his retreating figure as the rest of my "gang" faded out of the crowd around me.

"Did you get all that?" I asked out of the corner of my mouth.

"Two teams, neither one in this area. Shai-ster's running the show and therefore holding the bag," Tananda recited. "This area is both clear and under protection."

"Fat's Spaghetti Parlor is their headquarters, which is where we can find Shai-ster," Chumly completed. "Anything else?"

"Yeah," Aahz grinned. "Skeeve has a standing invite to drop by, and when he does, they're ready to tell him which team is working what area that day. Nice work."

"Lucky," I admitted with no embarrassment. "Well, shall we start?"

"Right," Aahz nodded. "Just like we planned, Tananda and Chumly are a team. Gus, you're with me. Skeeve and Massha, you start here. We all move out in different directions and space our hits so there's no pattern. Okay?"

"One more thing," I added. "Keep an eye on your disguises. I'm not sure of the exact range I can hold that spell at. If your disguise starts to fade, change direction to parallel mine."

"We meet back at the Yellow Crescent Inn," Gus finished. "And all of you watch your backs. I don't stock that much first aid gear."

"Good thought," I said. "Okay. Enough talk. Let's scatter and start giving the Mob a headache."

The other two teams had melted into the crowd of shoppers before I had even turned to Massha.

"Well, anything catch your eye for us to have a go at?"

"You know, you're starting to sound a bit like that troll."

That sounded a bit more abrupt than was Massha's normal style. I studied her curiously.

"Something bothering you?"

"Just a little nervous, I guess," she admitted. "Has it occurred to you all this plan has a major flaw? That to implement it potentially means getting the entire Bazaar after us, as well as the Mob?"

"Yes, it has."

"Doesn't it scare you?"

"Yes, it does."

"Well, how do you handle it?"

"By thinking about it as little possible," I said flatly. "Look, apprentice, aside from doing shtick in court for the amusement of the masses, this profession of ours is pretty dangerous. If we start dwelling on everything that can go wrong in the future, we'll either never move or blunder headlong into the present because our minds aren't on what we're doing right *now*. I try to be aware of the potential danger of a situation, but I don't worry about trouble until it happens. It's a little shaky, but it's worked so far."

"If you say so," she sighed. "Oh, well, gear me up and let's get started."

With a pass of my mind, I altered her features. Instead of being a massive woman, she was now a massive man . . . sort of. I had been experimenting with color lately, so I made her purple with reddish sideburns that ran all the way down her arms to her knuckles. Add some claw-like horns at the points of the ears and rough-textured, leathery skin on the face and hands, and you had a being *I* wouldn't want to mess with.

"Interesting," Massha grimaced, surveying what she could see of herself. "Did you make this up yourself, or is there a nasty dimension I haven't visited yet?"

"My own creation," I admitted. "The reputation you're going to build I wouldn't wish on any dimension I know of. Call it a Hoozit from the dimension Hoo."

"Who?"

"You've got it."

She rolled her eyes in exasperation.

"Hot stuff, do me a favor and only teach me magik, okay? Keep your sense of humor for yourself. I've already got enough enemies."

"We still need a target," I said, slightly hurt.

"How about that one? It looks breakable."

I looked where she was pointing and nodded.

"Good enough. Give me a twenty count head start. If they're not protected, I'll be back out. If you don't see me in twenty, they're fair game. Do your worst."

"You know," she smiled rubbing her hands together, "this could be fun."

"Just remember that *I'm* in there before you decide exactly what today's 'worst' is."

The display she had chosen was a small, three-sided tent with a striped top. It was lined with shelves that were crowded with an array of stoppered bottles of all sizes and colors. As I entered, I noticed there was something in each of the bottles—smoky things that shifted as if they were alive.

"May I help you, sahr?" The Deveel proprietor asked, baring what he doubtless thought was a winning smile.

"Just browsing," I yawned. "Actually, I'm seeking refuge from gossip. All anyone can talk about is this pack of ruffians that's selling insurance."

The Deveel's face darkened and he spat out the door.

"Insurance! Extortion I call it. They ruined two of my treasures before I could stop them long enough to subscribe to their services. It was a dark day when they first appeared at the Bazaar."

"Yes, yes. Believe me, I've heard it before."

Having established that this shop was indeed under

the protection of the Mob, I turned my attention to the displays.

With studied nonchalance, I plucked up a small bottle, no more than a hand's-width high, and peered at the contents. Murky movement and a vague sparkle met my gaze.

"Be careful," the proprietor cautioned. "Once a Djin is released, it can only be controlled if you address it by name."

"A Djin?"

The Deveel swept me with a speculative gaze. Since I wasn't doing the heavy work, I wasn't in disguise and looked like . . . well, me.

"I believe in Klah, they're referred to as Genies."

"Oh. You have quite a collection here."

The Deveel preened at the praise.

"Do not be fooled by the extent of my poor shop's selection, young sahr. They are extremely rare. I personally combed the far reaches of every dimension . . . at great personal expense, I might add . . . to find these few specimens worthy of. . . ."

I had been wondering when Massha was going to make her entrance. Well, she made it. Hoo-boy, did she make it. Right through the side of the tent.

With an almost musical chorus, the stand along the wall went over, dumping the bottles onto the floor. The released Djin rose in a cloud and poured out the open tent side, shrieking with inhuman joy as they went.

The Deveel was understandably upset.

"You idiot!" he shrieked. "What are you doing?"

"Pretty weak shelves," Massha muttered in a gravelly-bass voice.

"Weak shelves?"

"Sure. I mean, all I did was this . . ."

She shoved one of the remaining two shelves, which

toppled obligingly into the last display.

This time the Djin didn't even bother using the door. They streaked skyward, taking the top of the tent with them as they screamed their way to freedom.

"My stock! My tent! Who's going to pay for this?"

"That's Hoozit," Massha retorted, "and I'm certainly not going to pay. I don't have any money."

"No money?" the proprietor gasped.

"No. I just came in here to get out of the rain."

"Rain? Rain? But it isn't raining!"

"It isn't?" my apprentice blinked. "Then, good-bye."

With that she ambled off, making a hole in yet another tent side as she went.

The Deveel sank down in the shattered remains of his display and cradled his face in his hands.

"I'm ruined!" he moaned. "Ruined!"

"Excuse me for asking," I said. "But why didn't you call out their names and get them under control?"

"Call out their names? I can't remember the name of every Djin I collect. I have to look them up each time I sell one."

"Well, at least that problem's behind you."

That started him off again.

"Ruined!" he repeated needlessly. "What am I going to do?"

"I really don't know why you're so upset," I observed. "Weren't you just saying that you were insured?"

"Insured?"

The Deveel's head came up slowly.

"Certainly. You're paying to be sure things like this don't happen, aren't you? Well, it happened. It seems to me whoever's protecting your shop owes you an explanation, not to mention quite a bit of money."

"That's right!" the proprietor was smiling now. "More the latter than the former, but you're right!"

I had him going on now. All that was left to be done was the *coup de grace*.

"Tell you what. Just so your day won't be a total washout, I'll take this one. Now you won't have to stay open with just one Djin in stock."

I flipped him the smallest coin in my pouch. True to his heritage, he was sneering even as he plucked it out of the air.

"You can't be serious," he said. "This? For a Djin? That doesn't even cover the cost of the bottle!"

"Oh come, come, my good man," I argued. "We're both men of the world . . . or dimensions. We both know that's clear profit."

"It is?" he frowned.

"Of course," I said, gesturing at the broken glass on the floor. "No one can tell how many bottles were just broken. I know you'll just include this one on the list of lost stock and collect in full from your insurance in *addition* to what I just gave you. In fact, you could probably add five or six to the total if you were really feeling greedy."

"That's true," the Deveel murmured thoughtfully. "Hey, thanks! This might not turn out so bad after all."

"Don't mention it," I shrugged, studying the small bottle in my hand. "Now that we're in agreement on the price, though, could you look up the name of my Djin?"

"I don't have to. That one's new enough that I can remember. It's name is Kalvin."

"Kalvin?"

"Hey, don't laugh. It's the latest thing in Djins."

Chapter Seventeen:

"The best laid plans often go fowl."
—WILE E. COYOTE

"WELL, except for that, how are things going?"

"Except for that?" Shai-ster echoed incredulously.
"Except for that? Except for that things are going rot-
ten. This whole project is a disaster."

"Gee, that's tough," I said, with studied tones of
sympathy.

I had gotten to be almost a permanent fixture here at
Fat's Spaghetti Palace. Every night I dropped by to
check the troops' progress . . . theirs and mine.

It was nice to be able to track the effectiveness of your
activities by listening to the enemy gripe about them. It
was even nicer to be able to plan your next move by
listening to counter-attacks in the discussion stage.

"I still don't get it," Guido protested, gulping down
another enormous fork-full of spaghetti. "Everything
was goin' terrific at first. No trouble at all. Then
BOOM, it hits the fan, know what I mean?"

"Yeah! It was like someone was deliberately workin'
to put us out of business."

That last was from cousin Nunzio. For the longest

time I thought he was physically unable to talk. Once he got used to having me around, though, he opened up a little. In actuality, Nunzio was shy, a fact which was magnified by his squeaky little voice which seemed out of place coming from a muscleman.

"I warned you that Deveels can be a nasty lot," I said, eager to get the subject away from the possibility of organized resistance. "And if the shopkeepers are sneaky, it only stands to reason that the local criminal element would have to have a lot on the ball. Right, Guido?"

"That's right," the goon nodded vigorously, strands of spaghetti dangling from his mouth. "We criminal types can beat any honest citizen at anything. Say, did I ever tell you about the time Nunzio and me were . . ."

"Shut up, dummy!" Shai-ster snapped. "In case you haven't noticed, *we're* footing the bill for these local amateurs. We're getting our brains beat out financially, and it's up to you boys to catch up with the opposition and return the favor . . . physically."

"They're scared of us," Guido insisted. "Wherever we are, they aren't. If we can't find 'em, they can't be doin' *that* much damage."

"You know, brains never were your long suit, Guido," Shai-ster snarled. "Let me run this past you once real slow. So far, we've paid out six times as much as we've taken in. Add all our paychecks and expenses to that, and you might have a glimmer as to why the Big Boys are unhappy."

"But we haven't been collecting very long. After we've expanded our clientele . . ."

"Well be paying claims on that many more businesses," Shai-ster finished grimly. "Don't give me that 'we'll make it up on volume' guff. Either an operation is self-supporting *and* turning a profit from the beginning, or it's in trouble. And we're in trouble so deep, even if we could breathe through the tops of our heads we'd *still* be in trouble."

"Maybe if we got some more boys from back home. . . ." Nunzio began.

Shai-ster slapped his hand down on the table, stopping his lieutenant short.

"No more overhead!" he shouted. "I'm having enough trouble explaining our profit/loss statement to the Big Boys without the bottom line getting any worse. Not only are we not going to get any more help, we're going to start trimming our expenses, and I mean *right* now. Tell the boys to . . . what are *you* grinning at?"

This last was directed at me.

"Oh, nothing," I said innocently. "It's just that for a minute there you sounded just like someone I know back on Klah . . . name of Grimble."

"J.R. Grimble?" Shai-ster blinked.

Now it was my turn to be surprised.

"Why, yes. He's the Chancellor of the Exchequer back at Possiltum. Why, do you know him?"

"Sure. We went to school together. Chancellor of the Exchequer, huh? Not bad. If I had known he was working the court of Possiltum, I would have stuck around and said 'hi' when I was there."

Somehow, the thought of Shai-ster and Grimble knowing each other made me uneasy. There wasn't much chance of the two of them getting together and comparing notes, and even if they did, Grimble didn't know all that much about my *modus operandi*. Still, it served as a grim reminder that this was a very risky game I was playing, with some very dangerous people.

"I still think there's another gang out there somewhere,'' Nunzio growled. "There's too much going down for it to be independent operators.''

"You're half right," Shai-ster corrected. "There's too much going down for it to be a gang. Nobody's into that many things . . . not even us!''

"You lost me there, Shai-ster,'' I said, genuinely curious.

The mobster favored me with a patronizing smile.

"That's right. As a magician, you don't know that much about how organized crime works. Let me try to explain. When the Mob decides to move in, we hit one specialty field at a time . . . you know, like protection or the numbers. Like that. Focusing our efforts yields a better saturation as well as market penetration.''

"That makes sense," I nodded, not wanting to admit he had lost me again.

"Now you take a look at what's happening here. We're getting all sorts of claims; vandalism, shoplifting, armed robbery, even a couple cases of arson. It's too much of a mix to be the work of one group. We're dealing with a lot of small-time independents, and if we can make an example of a few of them, the others will decide there are easier pickings elsewhere.''

In a way, I was glad to hear this. I owed Aahz one more back-pat. He was the one who had decided that the efforts of our team were too limited. To accelerate our "crime wave," he had introduced the dubious practice of "insurance fraud" to Deva . . . and the Deveels were fast learners.

Is your stock moving too slow? Break it yourself and turn in a claim for vandalism. Trying to sell your shop, but nobody wants to buy, even at a discount? Torch the place and collect in full. Better still, want to fatten up your profit margin a little? Dummy up a few invoices and file a claim for "stolen goods." All profit, no cost.

The Deveels loved it. It let them make money and harass the Mob at the same time. No wonder Shai-ster's table was fast disappearing under a mountain of claims and protests.

It was terrific . . . except for the part about making an example out of everyone they caught. I made a mental note to warn the team about being extra careful.

"If it's not a gang, and they aren't working against us," Nunzio scowled, "why is everything happening in *our* areas? My dad taught me to be suspicious of coincidences. He got killed by one."

"How do you know it's just happening in our area?" Shai-ster countered. "Maybe we picked a bad area of the Bazaar to start our operation. Maybe the whole Bazaar is a bad area. Maybe we should have been suspicious when Skeeve here told us there were no police. You get this much money floating around with no police, of course there'll be crooks around."

"So what are we supposed to do?" Guido snarled, plucking his napkin from under his chin and throwing it on the table. "My boys can't be two places at once. We can't watch over our current clients and sign on new accounts, too."

"That's right," Shai-ster agreed, "so here's what we're going to do. First, we split up the teams. Two-thirds of the boys patrol the areas we've got under protection. The others go after new clients . . . *but* we don't just take anybody. We investigate and ask questions. We find out how much trouble a new area or a new shop has had *before* we take them as a client. Then we know who the bad risks are, and if we protect them at all, they pay double. *Capish?*"

Both Guido and Nunzio were thinking, and it was obvious the process hurt.

"I dunno," Nunzio squeaked at last. "Sumpin'

sounds kinda funny about that plan.''

"Crime wouldn't pay if the government ran it," I murmured helpfully.

"What's that?" Shai-ster snapped.

"Oh, just something my teacher told me once." I shrugged.

"Hey! Skeeve's right," Guido exclaimed.

"What you're sayin' is that we're going to be police-men and insurance investigators."

"Well, I wouldn't use those words. . . ."

" 'Well' nothin'. We ain't gonna do it!"

"Why not?"

"C'mon, Shai-ster. We're the bad guys. You know, crooks. What's it going to do to our reputation if it gets back to the Mob that we've turned into policemen?"

"They'll think we're valuable employees who are working hard to protect their investment."

"Yeah?" Guido frowned, unconvinced.

"Besides, it's only temporary," Shai-ster soothed. "Not only that, it's a smoke screen for what we'll *really* be doing."

"What's that?" I asked blandly.

Shai-ster shot a quick look around the restaurant, then leaned forward, lowering his voice.

"Well, I wasn't going to say anything, but remember that I was telling you about how the Mob focuses on one field at a time? The way I see it, maybe we picked the wrong field here at Deva. Maybe we shouldn't have tried the protection racket."

"So you're going to change fields?" I urged.

"Right," Shai-ster smiled. "We'll put the protection racket on slow-down mode for a while, and in the mean-time start leaning on the bookies."

"Now you're talking," Guido crowed. "There's always good money to be made at gambling."

"Keep your voice down, you idiot. It's supposed to be a secret."

"So who's to hear?" Guido protested.

"How about them?"

Shai-ster jerked his thumb toward a table of four enormous beings, alternately stuffing their faces and laughing uproariously.

"Them? That's the Hutt brothers. They're in here about once a week. They're too busy with their own games to bother us."

"Games? Are they gamblers?"

"Naw . . . well, except maybe Darwin. He's the leader of the pack. But he only gambles on businesses."

"Which one is he?"

"The thinnest one. I hear his fiancée has him on a diet. It's making him mean, but not dangerous to us."

Shai-ster turned back to our table.

"Well, keep your voice down anyway. How about it, Skeeve? The gambling, I mean. You've been here at the Bazaar before. Do you know any bookies we can get hold of?"

"Gee, the only one I know of for sure is the Geek," I said. "He's a pretty high-roller. If you boys are going to try to pull a fast one on him, though, don't tell him I was the one who singled him out."

Shai-ster gave me a broad wink.

"Gotcha. But anything we get from him, you're in for a percentage. You know, a finder's fee. We don't forget our friends."

"Gee, thanks," I managed, feeling more than a little guilty. "Well, I'd better be going. C'mon, Gleep."

"Gleep!" echoed my dragon, pulling his head up out of a tub of spaghetti at the sound of his name.

Fats had taken an instant liking to my pet, founded I suspect on Gleep's newfound capacity for the maggot-like stuff barely hidden by blood-red sauce that was the parlor's mainstay.

I had never been able to screw up my courage enough to try spaghetti, but my dragon loved it. Knowing some of the dubious things, edible and in, living and non, that also met with Gleep's culinary approval, this did little toward encouraging me to expand my dietary horizons to include this particular dish. Still, as long as I had Gleep along, we were welcome at Fats, even though my pet was starting to develop a waddle reminiscent of the parlor's proprietor.

"Say, Skeeve. Where do you keep your dragon during the day?"

I glanced over to find Shai-ster studying my pet through narrowed, thoughtful eyes.

"Usually he's with me, but sometimes I leave him with a dragon-sitter. Why?"

"I just remembered an 'interruption of business' claim we had to pay the other day . . . had to pay! Heck, we're still paying it. Anyway, this guy sells dragons, see, except for over a week now he hasn't sold a one. Usually sells about three a day and says since he paid us to be sure nothing happens to his business, we should make up the difference in his sales drop . . . and, you know, those things are *expensive*!"

"I know," I agreed, "but what does that have to do with Gleep?"

"Probably nothing. It's just that this guy swears that just before everything went to pot, some little dragon came by and talked to his dragons. Now they won't roar or blow fire or nothing. All they do is sleep and frolic . . . and who wants to buy a dragon that frolics, you know?"

"Talked to his dragons?" I asked uneasily.

For some reason, I had a sudden mental image of Gleep confronting Big Julie's dragon, a beast that dwarfed him in size, and winning.

"Well . . . they didn't exactly talk, but they did huddle up and put their heads together and made mumbly puffy noises at each other. Wouldn't let this guy near 'em until it was over. The only thing he's sure of is the little one, the one he says messed up his business, said something like 'Peep!' Said it a couple of times."

"Peep?" I said.

"Gleep!" answered my dragon.

Shai-ster stared at him again.

"C'mon, Shai-ster," Guido said, giving his superior a hearty shove. "Talking dragons? Somebody's pullin' your leg. Sounds to me like he got a bad shipment of dragons and is trying to get us to pay for them. Tell him to take a hike."

"It's not that easy," Shai-ster grumbled, "but I suppose you're right. I mean, all dragons look pretty much alike."

"True enough," I called, heading hastily for the nearest exit. "C'mon, Peep . . . I mean, Gleep!"

Maybe Shai-ster's suspicions had been lulled, but I still had a few of my own as we made our way back to the Yellow Crescent Inn.

"Level with me, Gleep. Did you do anything to louse up somebody's dragon business?"

"Gleep?" answered my pet in a tone exactly like my own when I'm trying too hard to sound innocent.

"Uh-huh. Well, stay out of this one. I think we've got it in hand without you getting in the line of fire."

"Gleep."

The answer was much more subdued this time, and I

realized he was drooping noticeably.

"Now don't sulk. I just don't want anything to happen to you. That's all."

I was suddenly aware that passers-by were staring at us. As strange as the Bazaar was, I guess they weren't used to seeing someone walking down the street arguing with a dragon.

"Let's hurry," I urged, breaking into a trot. "I don't know what we can do about the Mob moving in on the bookies, but I'm sure Aahz will think of something."

Chapter Eighteen:

"Life can be profitable, if you know the odds."

—RIPLEY

THE sports arena we were in was noticeably smaller than the stadium on Jahk where we had played in the Big Game, but no less noisy. Perhaps the fact that it was indoors instead of being open-air did something to the acoustics, but even at half-full the crowd in the arena made such a din I could barely hear myself think.

Then again, there was the smell. The same walls and ceiling that botched up the acoustics did nothing at all for ventilation. Even a few thousand beings from assorted dimensions in these close quarters produced a blend of body odors that had my stomach doing slow rolls . . . or maybe it was just my nerves.

"Could you explain to me again about odds?"

"Not now," the Geek snarled, nervously playing with his program. "I'm too busy worrying."

"I'll give it a try, hot stuff," Massha volunteered from my other side. "Maybe I can say it in less technical jargon than our friend here."

"I'd appreciate it," I admitted.

139

That got me a black look from the Geek, but Massha was already into it.

"First, you've got to understand that for the most part, bookies aren't betting their own money. They're acting as agents or go-betweens for people who are betting different sides of the same contest. Ideally, the money bet on each side evens out, so the bookie himself doesn't have any of his own money riding on the contest."

"Then how do they make their money?"

"Sometimes off a percentage, sometimes . . . but that's another story. What we're talking about is odds. Okay?"

"I guess so," I shrugged.

"Now, the situation I described is the ideal. It assumes the teams or fighters or whatever are evenly matched. That way, some people bet one side, some the other, but overall it evens out. That's even odds or 1-1."

She shifted her weight a bit, ignoring the glares from our fellow patrons when the entire row of seats wobbled in response.

"But suppose things were different. What if, instead of an even match, one side had an advantage . . . like say if Badaxe were going to fight King Rodrick?"

"That's easy," I smiled. "Nobody would be on the King."

"Precisely," Massha nodded. "Then everybody would bet one side, and the bookies would have to cover all the bets with their own money . . . bets they stood a good chance of losing."

"So they don't take any bets."

"No. They rig things so that people will bet on the king."

I cocked an eyebrow at her.

"They could try, but I sure wouldn't throw my gold away like that. I'd back Badaxe."

"Really?" Massha smiled. "What if, instead of betting one gold piece to win one gold piece, you had to bet ten gold pieces on Badaxe to win one back?"

"Well . . ."

"Let me make it a little harder. How about if you bet one gold piece on the King, and he won, that instead of getting one gold piece back, you got a hundred?"

"I . . . um . . . might take a long shot on the King," I said, hesitantly. "There's always a chance he could get lucky. Besides, if I lose, I'm only out one gold piece."

". . . And *that's* how bookies use odds to cover themselves. Now, how they figure out how many bets they need on the King at 'x' odds to cover the bets they have on Badaxe at 'y' odds is beyond me."

I looked at the Deveel next to me with new respect.

"Gee, Geek. I never really realized how complicated your work is."

The Deveel softened a bit. They're as susceptible to flattery as anyone else.

"Actually, it's even more complicated than that," he admitted modestly. "You've got to keep track of several contests at once, sometimes even use the long bets from one to cover the short bets on another. Then there are side bets, like who will score how often in which period in the Big Game. It isn't easy, but a sharp being can make a living at it."

"So what are the odds tonight?"

The Deveel grimaced.

"Lousy. It's one of those Badaxe and the King matchups, if I was following your example right. In this case, the team you'll see in red trunks are Badaxe.

They're hotter than a ten dollar laser and have won their last fifteen bouts. The weak sisters . . . the King to you . . . will be in white trunks and haven't won a bout in two years. When the Mob put their bet down, the odds were running about two hundred to one against the whites.''

I whistled softly.

"Wow. Two hundred in gold return on a one-gold-piece bet. Did you remember to act surprised when they put their money down?"

"I didn't have to act," the Geek said through tight lips. "Not with the size bet they came up with. Being forewarned, I had expected they wouldn't be going small, but still . . ."

He shook his head and lapsed into silence.

I hadn't really paused to consider the implication of the odds, but I did now. If betting one piece could get you two hundred back, then a bet of a thousand would have a potential payback of two hundred thousand! And a ten thousand bet . . .

"How big was their bet?" I asked fearfully.

"Big enough that if I lose, I'll be working for the Mob for the rest of my life to pay it off . . . and Deveels don't have short life-spans."

"Wait a minute. Didn't Aahz tell you that if you lost, we'd cover it out of our expense money?"

"He did," the Deveel said. "And he also pointed out that if you were covering my losses, you'd also take all winnings if things went as planned. I opted to take the risk, and the winnings, myself."

Massha leaned forward to stare.

"Are you that confident, or that greedy?"

"More the latter," the Geek admitted. "Then again, I got burnt rather badly betting against Skeeve here in the Big Game. I figure it's worth at least one pass backing the shooter who's working a streak.''

I shook my head in puzzlement.

"Aren't you afraid of losing?"

"Well, it did occur to me that it might be me and not the Mob who's being set up here. That's why I'm sitting next to you. If this turns out to be a double cross . . .''

"You're pretty small to be making threats, Geek," Massha warned.

". . . And you're too big to dodge fast if I decide I'm being had,'' the Deveel shot back.

"Knock it off, both of you," I ordered. "It's academic anyway. There won't be any problems . . . or if there are, I'll be as surprised as you are, Geek.''

"More surprised, I hope," the Deveel sneered. "I'm half expecting this to blow up, remember?"

"But Aahz has assured me that the fix is in."

"Obviously. Otherwise, the Mob wouldn't be betting so heavily. The question is, which fix is going to work, theirs or yours?"

Just then a flurry of activity across the arena caught my eye. The Mob had just arrived . . . in force. Shai-ster was there, flanked by Guido and Nunzio and backed by the remaining members of the two teams currently assigned to the Bazaar. Seen together and moving, as opposed to individually feeding their faces at Fats', they made an impressive group. Apparently others shared my opinion. Even though they were late, no one contested their right to prime seats as they filed into the front row. In fact, there was a noticeable bailing out from the desired seats as they approached.

It was still a new enough experience for me to see other beings I knew in a crowd at the Bazaar that I stood up and waved at them before I realized what I was doing. Then it dawned on me! If they saw me sitting with the Geek and then lost a big bet, they might put two and two together and get five!

I stopped waving and tried to ease back into my seat, but it was too late. Guido had spotted my gyrations and nudged Shai-ster to point me out. Our eyes met and he nodded acknowledgement before returning to scanning the crowd.

Crestfallen, I turned to apologize to the Geek, only to find myself addressing a character with a pasty complexion and hairy ears who bore no resemblance at all to the Deveel who had been sitting beside me.

I almost . . . almost! . . . looked around to see where the Geek had gone. Then I did a little mental arithmetic and figured it out.

A disguise spell!

I'd gotten so used to fooling people myself with that spell that when someone did the same to me, I was completely taken in.

"Still kinda new at this intrigue stuff, aren't you?" he observed dryly from his new face.

Fortunately I was saved the problem of thinking up a suitable response by the entrance of the contestants. With the scramble of planning and launching our counter-offensive, I hadn't really been briefed on what the Mob was betting on except that it would be a tag-team wrestling match. No one said what the contestants would be like, and I had assumed it would be like the matches I had seen back on Klah. I should have known better.

The two teams were made up of beings who barely stood high enough to reach my waist! I mean they were *small!* They looked like kids . . . if you're used to having kids around with four arms each.

"What are those?" I demanded.

"Those are the teams," the Geek said helpfully.

"I mean, *what* are they? Where are they from?"

"Oh. Those are Tues."

"And you bet on them? I mean, I've heard of midget wrestling, but this is ridiculous!"

"Don't knock it," the Deveel shrugged. "They're big on the wrestling circuit. In fact, teams like this are their dimension's most popular export. Everyone knows them as the Terrible Tues. They're a lot more destructive than you'd guess from their size."

"This is a put-on, right?"

"If you really want to see something, you should catch their other export. It's a traveling dance troupe called the Tue Tours."

Massha dropped a heavy hand on my shoulder.

"Hot stuff, remember our deal about my lessons?"

"Later, Massha. The match is about to start."

Actually, it was about to finish. It was that short, if you'll pardon the expression.

The first member of the favored red trunk team simply strolled out and pinned his white-trunked rival. Though the pin looked a bit like someone trying to wrap a package with tangled string, the red-trunker made it seem awfully easy. All efforts of his opponent's partner to dislodge the victor were in vain, and the bout was over.

"Well, that's that," the Geek said, standing up. "A pleasure doing business with you, Skeeve. Look me up again if you tie on to a live one."

"Aren't you going to collect your bet?"

The Deveel shrugged.

"No rush. Besides, I think your playmates are a little preoccupied just now."

I looked where he was pointing and saw Shai-ster storming toward the dressing rooms with Guido and

Nunzio close behind. None of them looked particularly happy, which was understandable, given the circumstances.

"Whoops. That's my cue. See you back at the Yellow Crescent, Massha."

And with that, I launched myself in an interceptor course with the angry mobsters.

Chapter Nineteen:

"These blokes need to be taught to respect their superiors."

—GEN. CORNWALLIS

I ALMOST missed them. Not that I was moving slow, mind you. It's just that they had a real head of steam on.

"Hi guys!" I called, just as Shai-ster was raising a fist to hammer on the dressing room door. "Are you going to congratulate the winners, too?"

Three sets of eyes bored into me as my "friends" spun around.

"Congratulate!" Guido snarled. "I'll give 'em congratulate."

"Wait a minute," Shai-ster interrupted. "What did you mean, 'too'?"

"Well, that's why *I'm* here. I just won a sizable bet on the last match."

"How sizable?"

"Well, sizable for me," I qualified. "I stand to collect fifty gold pieces."

"Fifty," Guido snorted. "You know how much we *lost* on that fiasco?"

"Lost?" I frowned. "Didn't you know the Reds were favored?"

"Of course we knew," Shai-ster snarled. "That's why we were set to make a killing when they lost."

"But what made you think they were going to . . . Oh! Was that what you were talking about when you said you were going into gambling?"

"That's right. The red team was supposed to take a graceful dive in the third round. We paid them enough . . . more than enough, actually."

He sounded so much like Grimble I couldn't resist taking a cheap shot.

"Judging from the outcome, it sounds to me that you paid them a little less than enough."

"It's not funny. Now, instead of recouping our losses, we've got *another* big loss to explain to the Big Boys."

"Oh come on, Shai-ster," I smiled. "How much can it cost to fix a fight?"

"Not much," he admitted. "But when you figure in the investment money we just lost, it comes to. . . ."

"Investment money?"

"He means the bet," Guido supplied.

"Oh. Well, I suppose that's the risk you take when you try to make a killing."

An evil smile flitted across Shai-ster's face.

"Oh, we're going to make a killing, all right," he said. "It's time the locals at this Bazaar learned what it means to cross the Mob."

With that, he nodded at Guido who opened the dressing room door.

All four wrestlers were sharing the same room, and they looked up expectantly as we filed in. That's right. I said we. I kind of tagged along at the end of the procession and no one seemed to object.

"Didn't you clowns forget something out there?" Shai-ster said for his greeting. "Like who was supposed to win?"

The various team members exchanged glances. Then the smallest of the red team shrugged.

"Big deal. So we changed our minds."

"Yeah," his teammate chimed in. "We decided it would be bad for our image to lose . . . especially to these stumblebums."

That brought the white team to its feet.

"Stumblebums?" one of them bellowed. "You caught us by surprise, that's all. We was told to take it easy until the third round."

"If you took it any easier, you'd be asleep. We were supposed to be wrestling, not dancing."

Shai-ster stepped between them.

"So you all admit you understood your original instructions?"

"Hey, get off our backs, okay? You'll get your stinking money back, so what's your beef, anyway?"

"Even if you gave us a full refund," Shai-ster said softly, "there's still a matter of the money we lost betting on you. I don't suppose any of you are independently wealthy?"

"Oh, sure," one of the reds laughed. "We're just doin' this for kicks."

"I thought not. Guido. Nunzio. See what you can do about squaring accounts with these gentlemen. And take your time. I want them to feel it, you know?"

"I dunno, Shai-ster," Guido scowled. "They're awfully small. I don't think we can make it last too long."

"Well, do your best. Skeeve? Would you join me outside? I don't think you're going to want to see this."

He was closer to being right than he knew. Even

though I had been through some rough and tumble times during recent years, that didn't mean I enjoyed it—even to watch.

The door was barely shut behind us when a series of thuds and crashes erupted inside. It was painful just to listen to, but it didn't last long.

"I told them to take their time," Shai-ster said, scowling at the silence. "Oh well, I guess . . ."

The door opened, revealing one of the white team.

"If you've got any more lessons out there, I suggest you send them in. These two didn't teach us much at all."

He shut the door again, but not before we caught a glimpse of the two bodyguards unconscious on the floor. Well, Guido was on the floor. Nunzio was kind of standing on his head in the corner.

"Tough little guys," I remarked casually. "It must be the four arms. Think you could find work for them in the Mob?"

Shai-ster was visibly shaken, but he recovered quickly.

"So they want to play rough. Well, that's fine by me."

"You aren't going in there alone, are you?" I asked, genuinely concerned.

He favored me with a withering glance.

"Not a chance."

With that, he put his fingers in his mouth and blew a loud blast. At least, that's what it looked like. I didn't *hear* a thing.

Before I could ask what he was doing, though, a thunder of footsteps announced the arrival of two dozen Mob reinforcements.

Neat trick. I guess the whistle had been too high for me to hear . . . or too low.

"They got Guido and Nunzio," Shai-ster shouted before the heavies had come to a complete halt. "Let's show 'em who's running things around here. Follow me!"

Jerking the door open, he plunged into the dressing room with the pack at his heels.

I'm not sure if Shai-ster had ever actually been in a fight before, much less led a team into a fight. I *am*, however, sure he never tried it again.

The screams of pain and anguish that poured out of that room moved me to take action. I walked a little further down the hall and did my waiting there. It turned out my caution was needless. The wall didn't collapse, nor did the ceiling or the building itself. Several hunks of plaster did come loose, however, and at one point someone poked a hole in the wall . . . with his head.

It occurred to me that if the fight fans in the arena *really* wanted to get their money's worth, they should be down here. Additional thought made me decide it was just as well they didn't. There were already more than enough beings crowded into that dressing room . . . which was as good a reason as any for my staying in the hall.

Eventually the sounds of battle died away, leaving only ominous silence. I reminded myself that I had every confidence in the outcome. As the length of silence grew, I found it necessary to remind myself several times.

Finally the door opened, and the four Tues filed out laughing and chatting together.

"Cute," I called. "Don't hurry or anything. I can worry out here all day."

One of the white team ran up and gave me a hug and a kiss.

"Sorry, handsome. We were having so much fun we forgot about you."

"Um . . . could you do something about the disguises before you kiss me again?"

"Whoops. Sorry about that!"

The taller red team member closed his eyes, and the Tues were gone. In their places stood Aahz, Gus, Tananda, and Chumly. That's why I hadn't been worried . . . much.

"Nice work, Gus," I said, nodding my approval. "But I still think I could have handled the disguises myself."

"Have you ever seen a Tue before?" Aahz challenged.

"Well . . . no."

"Gus has. That's why he handled the disguises. End of discussion."

"Used to have a secretary named Etheyl," the gargoyle explained, ignoring Aahz's order. "She was a big fan of the wrestling circuit."

"A secretary?" I blinked.

"Sure, haven't you ever heard of a Tue Fingered Typist?"

"Enough!" Aahz insisted, holding up his hand. "I vote we head back to the Yellow Crescent Inn for a little celebration. I think we've thwarted the Mob enough for one night."

"Yeah," Tananda grinned. "That'll teach 'em to pick on someone their own size."

"But you are their size," I frowned.

"I know," she winked. "That's the point."

"I say, are you sure, Aahz?" Chumly interjected. "I mean, we gave them a sound thrashing, but will it hold them until morning?"

"If they're lucky," my mentor grinned. "Remember,

once they wake up, they're going to have to report in to their superiors."

"Do you think they'll try to recoup their losses with another stab at gambling?" I asked.

"I hope so," Aahz said, his grin getting broader. "The next big betting event on the docket is the unicorn races, and we've got that covered easily."

"You mean Buttercup? You can't enter him in a race. He's a war-unicorn."

"I know. Think about it."

Chapter Twenty:

"Figure the last thing you would expect the enemy to do, then count on him doing precisely that!"

—RICHELIEU

THE Mob did not try another gambit right after their disastrous attempt to move in on Deva's bookies. In fact, for some time afterward, things were quiet . . . too quiet, as Aahz put it.

"I don't like it," he declared, staring out the front window of the Yellow Crescent Inn. "They're up to something. I can feel it."

"Fats says they haven't been around for nearly a week," I supplied. "Maybe they've given up."

"Not a chance. There's got to be at least one more try, if for nothing else than to save face. And instead of getting ready, we're sitting around on our butts."

He was right. For days now, the team's main activity had been hanging around Gus's place waiting for some bit of information to turn up. Our scouting missions had yielded nothing, so we were pretty much reduced to relying on the normal Bazaar gossip network to alert us to any new Mob activity.

"Be reasonable, Aahz," Chumly protested. "We can't plan or prepare without any data to work with.

You've said yourself that action in an absence of information is wasted effort, eh what? Makes the troops edgy.''

Aahz stalked over to where the troll was sprawled.

"Don't start quoting me at me! You're the one who usually argues with everything I say. If everybody starts agreeing with me, we aren't using all the mental resources we can.''

"But you're the one saying that we should be planning,'' I pointed out.

"Right,'' my mentor smiled. "So we might as well get started. In absence of hard facts, we'll have to try to second-guess them. Now, where is the Bazaar most vulnerable to Mob takeover? Tananda, have you seen . . . Tananda?''

She abandoned her window-gazing to focus on the discussion.

"What was that, Aahz? Sorry. I was watching that Klahd coming down the street dressed in bright purple.''

"Purple?''

Massha and I said it together.

I started to race her for the window, then changed my mind. What if I won? I didn't want to be between the window and her mass when she finally got there. Instead, I waited until she settled into position, then eased in beside her.

"That's him all right,'' I said out loud, confirming my unvoiced thoughts. "That's Don Bruce. Well, now we know what the Mob's been doing. They've been whistling up the heavy artillery. The question is, what is he doing here at the Bazaar? When we get the answer to that, we'll be able to plan our next move.''

"Actually, the question should be what is he doing here at the Yellow Crescent Inn,'' Gus commented dryly from my elbow. "And I think we're about to get the answer.''

Sure enough, Don Bruce was making a beeline for the very building we were watching him from. With his walk, it had taken me a minute to zero in on his direction.

"All right. We know who he is and that he's coming here. Now, let's quit gawking like a bunch of tourists."

Aahz was back in his familiar commander role again. Still, I noticed he was no quicker to leave the window than any of the rest of us.

"Everybody sit down and act natural. Skeeve, when he gets here, let me do the talking, okay?"

"Not a chance, Aahz," I said, sinking into a chair. "He's used to dealing with me direct. If we try to run in a middleman he'll know something's up. Sit at this table with me, though. I'm going to need your advice on this one."

By the time Don Bruce opened the door, we were all sitting. Aahz and I at one table, and two others accommodating Massha and Gus, and the Chumly-Tananda team respectively. I noticed that we had left two-thirds of the place empty to sit at adjoining tables, which might have looked a little suspicious. I also noticed we had reflexively split up into two-person teams again, but it was too late to correct either situation.

"Hi there," Don Bruce called, spotting me at once. "Thank goodness I found you here. This Bazaar is great fun to wander, but simply *beastly* at finding what or who you're looking for."

"You were looking for me?"

This was not the best news I had heard all day. Despite his affected style of speech, I had a healthy respect for Don Bruce. From what I had seen of the Mob, it was a rough group, and I figured no one could hold down as high a position as Don Bruce did, unless there was some real hard rock under that soft exterior. Friendly greeting or not, I began to feel the fingers of cold fear gripping my stomach.

"That's right. I've *got* to have a meet with you, you know? I *was* hoping I could speak with you in private."

The last thing in the world I wanted right now was to be alone with Don Bruce.

"It's all right," I said expansively. "These are my friends. Any business I have with your . . . organization we're in on together . . . I mean, can be discussed in front of them."

"Oh, very well."

The Mob chieftain flounced onto a chair at my table.

"I didn't mean to be rude, and I *do* want to meet you all. It's just that, first thing, there are some pressing matters to deal with."

"Shoot," I said, then immediately wished I had chosen another word.

"Well, you know we're trying to move in on this place, and you know it hasn't been going well . . . no, don't deny it. It's true. Shai-ster has mentioned you often in his reports, so I know how well informed you are."

"I haven't seen Shai-ster lately, but I do know he's been working hard at the project."

"That's right," Aahz chimed in. "From what Skeeve's been telling us, Shai-ster is a good man. If he can't pull it off, you might as well pack up and go home."

"He's an idiot!" Don Bruce roared, and for a moment we could see the steel inside the velvet glove. "The reason you haven't seen him is that I've pulled him from the project completely. He thought we should give up, too."

"You aren't giving up?" I said, fearfully.

"I can't. Oh, if you only knew what I go through on the Council. I made such a thing out of this Deva project and how much it could do for the Mob. If we pulled out now, it would be the same as saying I don't know a good thing when I see it. No sir. Call it family politics or stubborn pride, we're going to stay right here."

My heart sank.

"But if the operation is losing money—" I began, but he cut me off with a gesture.

"So far . . . but not for long. You see, I've figured out for myself what's going wrong here."

"You have? How? I mean, this is your first visit here since the project started."

I was starting to sweat a bit. Don Bruce was regarding me with an oily reptilian smile I didn't like at all.

"I saw it in the reports," he declared. "Clear as the nose on your face. That's why I know Shai-ster's an idiot. The problem was right here in front of him and he couldn't see it. That problem is you."

My sweat turned cold. At the edge of my vision I saw Tananda run her fingers through her hair, palming one of her poison darts in the process, and Massha was starting to play with her rings. Chumly and Gus exchanged glances, then shifted in their chairs slightly. Of our entire team, only Aahz seemed unconcerned.

"You'll have to be a little clearer for the benefit of us slow folks," he drawled. "Just how do you figure that Skeeve here is a problem?"

"Look at the facts," Don Bruce said, holding up his fingers to tick off the count.

"He's been here the whole time my boys were having trouble; he knows the Bazaar better than my boys; he knows magik enough to do things my boys can't handle; and now I find out he's got a bunch of friends and contacts here."

"So?" my mentor said softly.

"So? Isn't it obvious? The problem with the operation is that he should have been working for us all along."

By now I had recovered enough to have my defense ready.

"But just because I . . . what?"

"Sure. That's why I'm here. Now I know you said before you didn't want to work for the Mob full time. That's why I'm ready to talk a new deal with you. I want you to run the Mob's operation here at the Bazaar . . . and I'm willing to pay top dollar."

"How much is that in gold?"

Aahz was leaning forward now.

"Wait a minute! Whoa! Stop!" I interrupted. "You can't be serious. I don't have the time or the know-how to make this a profitable project."

"It doesn't have to be profitable," Don argued. "Break even would be nice, or even just lose money slower. Anything to get the council to look elsewhere for things to gripe about at our monthly Meetings. You could do it in your extra time."

I started to say something, but Aahz put a casual hand on my shoulder. I knew that warning. If I tried to interrupt or correct him, that grip would tighten until my bones creaked.

"Now let me see if I've got this right," he said, showing *all* his teeth. "You want my man here to run your operation, but you don't care if it doesn't show a profit?"

"That's right."

"Of course, with things as shaky as they are now, you'd have to guarantee his salary."

Don Bruce pursed his lips and looked at me.

"How much does he cost?"

"Lots," Aahz confided. "But less than the total salary of the force you've got here now."

"Okay. He's worth it."

"Aahz . . ." I began, but the grip on my shoulder tightened.

". . . *And* you aren't so much concerned with the Mob's reputation here on Deva as you are with how the Council treats you, right?"

"Well . . . yeah. I guess so."

". . . So he'd have free rein to run the operation the way he saw fit. No staff forced on him or policies to follow?"

"No. I'd have to at least assign him a couple bodyguards. Anybody running a Mob operation has got to have a couple of the Family's boys to be sure nothing happens to him."

Aahz scowled.

"But he's already got . . ."

"How about Guido and Nunzio?" I managed, through gritted teeth.

Abruptly the grip on my shoulder vanished.

"Those losers?" Don Bruce frowned. "I was going to have a severe talk with them after this disaster, but if you want 'em, they're yours."

". . . But since *you're* the one insisting on them, they don't show up on *our* overhead. Right?" Aahz said firmly.

I leaned back, working my shoulder covertly, and tried to ignore the horrified stares my friends were exchanging. I didn't know for sure what Aahz was up to, but knew better than to get in his way when he smelled money.

I could only cross my fingers and hope that he knew what he was doing . . . for a change.

Chapter Twenty-One:

"Stayin' alive! Stayin' alive!"

—V. DRACULA

THE representatives of the Bazaar Merchants didn't look happy, but then Deveels never do when they're parting with money.

"Thank you gentlemen," Aahz beamed, rubbing his hands together gleefully over the substantial pile of gold on the table.

"You're sure the Mob is gone?" the head spokesman asked, looking plaintively at the gold.

"Positive. We've broken their reign of terror and sent them packing."

The Deveel nodded.

"Good. Now that that's settled, we'll be going."

". . . Of course," Aahz yawned, "there's no guarantee they won't be back tomorrow."

That stopped the delegation in their tracks.

"What? But you said . . ."

"Face it, gentlemen. Right now, the only thing between the Mob and the Bazaar is the Great Skeeve here, and once he leaves . . ."

The Deveels exchanged glances.

"I don't suppose you'd consider staying," one said hopefully.

I favored him with a patronizing smile.

"I'd love to, but you know how it is. Expenses are high, and I've got to keep moving to eke out a living."

"But with your reputation, clients will be looking for you. What you really need is a permanent location so you can be found."

"True enough," Aahz smiled. "But to be blunt, why should we give you for free what other dimensions are willing to pay for? I should think that if anybody could understand that, you Deveels would."

"Now we're getting to the heart of the matter," the lead spokesman sighed, pulling up a chair. "Okay. How much?"

"How much?" Aahz echoed.

"Don't give me that," the Deveel snapped. "Innocence looks ridiculous on a Pervert. Just tell us what kind of retainer would be necessary to keep the Great Skeeve around as the Bazaar's magician in residence."

Aahz winked at me.

"I'm sure you'll find his fee reasonable," he said. "Well, reasonable when you stop to think what you're getting for your money. Of course, the figure I'm thinking of is just for making the Bazaar his base of operations. If any specific trouble arises, we'll have to negotiate that separately."

"Of course," the Deveel winced.

I settled back to wait patiently. This was going to take a while, but I was confident of the eventual outcome. I also knew that whatever fee Aahz was thinking of originally just got doubled when the Deveel made that 'Pervert' crack. As a Pervect, Aahz is very sensitive about how he's addressed . . . and this time I wasn't about to argue with him.

"I love it!" Aahz crowed, modestly. "Not only are we getting a steady income from both the Mob and the Deveels, we don't have to do a thing to earn it! This is even better than the setup we had at Possiltum."

"It's a sweet deal, Aahz."

"And how about this layout? It's a far cry from that shack you and Garkin were calling home when we first met."

Aahz and I were examining our new home, provided as an extra clause in our deal with the Bazaar merchants. It was huge, rivaling the size of the Royal Palace at Possiltum. The interesting thing was that from the outside it looked no bigger than an average Bazaar stall.

"Of course, holding out for a lifetime discount on anything at the Bazaar was a stroke of genius, if I do say so myself."

"Yeah, Aahz. Genius."

My mentor broke off his chortling and self-congratulations to regard me quizzically.

"Is something bothering you, Skeeve? You seem a little subdued."

"It's nothing, really."

"Come on. Out with it," he insisted. "You should be on top of the world right now, not moping around like you just heard that your dragon has a terminal illness or something."

"Well, it's a couple of things," I admitted grudgingly. "First, I've got a bad feeling about those deals you just put together."

"Now wait a minute," my mentor scowled. "We talked all this out before we went after the merchants and you said that double-dealing wouldn't bother you."

"It doesn't. If anything, I'm glad to see both the Mob and the Deveels getting a little of their own back for a change."

"Then what's wrong? I got you everything I could think of!"

"That's what's wrong."

My mentor shook his head sharply as if to clear his vision.

"I've got to admit, this time *you* lost *me*. Could you run that one past again, slow?"

"Come on, Aahz. You know what I'm talking about. You've gotten me more money than I could spend in a lifetime, a beautiful house . . . not just anywhere, mind you, but at the Bazaar itself . . . steady work anytime I want it . . . in short, everything I need to not only survive, but prosper. Everything."

"So?"

"So are you setting me up so you can leave? Is that what this is all about?"

I had secretly hoped that Aahz would laugh in my face and tell me I was being silly. Instead, he averted his eyes and lapsed into silence.

"I've been thinking about it," he said finally. "You're doing pretty well lately and, like you say, this latest deal will insure you won't starve. The truth of the matter is that you really don't need me anymore."

"But Aahz!"

"Don't 'but Aahz' me! All I'm doing is repeating what you shoved down my throat at the beginning of this caper. You don't need me. I've been giving it a lot of thought, and you're right. I thought you always wanted to hear me say that."

"Maybe I don't like being right," I said plaintively.

"Maybe I wish I *did* need you more and things could go on forever like they have in the past."

"That's most of growing up, kid," Aahz sighed. "Facing up to reality whether we like it or not. You've been doing it, and I figure it's about time I did the same. That's why I'm going to stick around."

"But you don't have to . . . what?"

My mentor's face split in one of his expansive grins.

"In this case, the reality that I'm facing is that whether you need me or not, I've had more fun since I took you on as an apprentice than I've had in centuries. I'm not sure exactly what's going to happen to you next, but I wouldn't miss it for all the gold on Deva."

"That's great!"

". . . Of course, there's still a lot I can teach you, just like there's a lot I have to learn from you."

"From me?" I blinked.

"Uh huh. I've been learning from you for some time now, kid. I was just never up to admitting it before. You've got a way of dealing with people that gets you respect, even from the ones who don't like you. I haven't always been able to get that. Lots of folks are afraid of me, but not that many respect me. That's why I've been studying your methods, and have every intention of continuing."

"That's . . . umm . . . interesting, Aahz. But how come you're telling me this now?"

"Because if I stay around, it'll be on one condition: that you wake up and accept the fact that you're a full partner in our relationship. No more of this 'apprentice' crud. It's getting too rough on my nerves."

"Gee, Aahz . . . I . . ."

"Deal?"

"Deal."

We shook hands solemnly, and I remembered he had refused this simple act when he first accepted me as an apprentice. A full partner. Wow!

"Now what's the other thing?"

"Hmm, excuse me?"

"If I recall correctly, you said there were a couple of things bothering you. What's the other?"

"Well . . . it's this house."

"What about the house?" Aahz exploded, slipping easily back into his old patterns. "It's got enough room for us *and* our friends *and* your bodyguards when they show up *and* Buttercup and Gleep and anyone else who wanders by."

"That's true."

"What's more, we got it for free. It's a good deal."

"Say that again, Aahz."

"I said, 'it's a good . . . 'Oh."

"From the Deveels, right?"

"Oh come on, Skeeve. It's just a house. What could be wrong?"

"To use your phrase, 'The mind boggles.' I've been trying to spot the catch, and I want you to check me to see if my facts and logic are correct."

"Okay."

"Now. Deveels are experts at dimension travel. If I understand it right, they manage these 'bigger inside than outside' houses by offsetting the dimensions just a bit. That is, if we numbered the dimensions, and Deva was one, then our door is in dimension one and the rest of our house is in dimension one point four or something."

"Now *that's* one I hadn't thought about before," Aahz admitted. "The Deveels have been pretty tight-lipped about it. Makes sense, though. It would be rough to play the poverty-stricken shopowner with a place like this just over your shoulder. If I had thought about it I would have realized a Deveel needs someplace secret to keep his wealth.''

''So we've effectively been given our own dimension,'' I continued; ''An unlisted dimension that's all ours. For free, no less.''

''That's right,'' Aahz nodded, but there was a note of doubt in his voice now.

''What I wonder about is how many of these offset dimensions do the Deveels have access to, and why is this particular one standing vacant? What's in this dimension?''

''Our house?'' my mentor suggested tentatively.

''And what else?'' I urged. ''I've noticed there are no windows. What's outside our back door that the Deveels were so eager to give away?''

''Back door?''

I pulled away the tapestry to reveal the door I had spotted during our first tour. It was heavy wood with strange symbols painted on it. It also had a massive beam guarding it, and several smaller but no less effective-looking locks around the edge.

''I tried to say something at the time, but you kept telling me to shut up.''

''I did, didn't I.''

We both stared at the door in silence for several minutes.

''Tell you what,'' Aahz said softly. ''Let's save investigating this for another day.''

''Right,'' I agreed, without hesitation.

''. . . And until we do, let's not mention this to the others.''

''My thoughts precisely.''

"... And, partner?"

"Yes, Aahz?"

"If anyone knocks at this door, don't answer unless I'm with you."

Our eyes met, and I let the tapestry fall back into place.